Sign up for our newsletter to hear about
new releases, read interviews with
authors, enter giveaways, and more.

www.ylva-publishing.com

THE SET
Piece
CATHERINE LANE

To Peggy, who should be here to read this

ACKNOWLEDGMENTS

How lucky am I? I got to work with the very best right out of the gate. Golden Crown Literary Society opened the door with its incredible mentor program and in walked Jae, the best-selling author. Her instruction was patient, generous, and invaluable, and I know that I would not be on this journey if it weren't for her.

My editor, Gill McKnight, pushed me when she needed to and spoiled me when she could. The story is certainly better for her careful attention, thank you.

And finally Astrid Ohletz and her amazing team at Ylva Publishing, who took a chance and then supported me every step of the way.

Of course, my family is also some of the very best people I know. My wife and son always believed in me even when we all realized what I had gotten us into. Writing is so much easier when I have the wind of their love at my back.

And then there is soccer, the best game in the world! It gave me a wonderful childhood, an introduction to my wife, and the inspiration for this novel!

CHAPTER 1

THE LOS ANGELES ATOMS' MIDFIELDER rushed toward the left corner of the soccer field, the ball glued to his feet. He cut around a defender and sent a lovely precision pass into the middle of the penalty area. Diego Torres, star forward of the Atoms, hunky underwear model, and all-around great guy, collected the ball with an outstretched foot. His brilliant first touch sent both defenders guarding him in the wrong direction and left the goalie exposed to the blistering shot that was surely only seconds away.

The crowd jumped to its feet, ready to cheer the goal.

Torres's foot met the ball with a thunderous clap. It spun, like the charged atom it was dyed to resemble, and sailed toward the left-hand corner. And then, unbelievably, continued to drift wide, hitting the retaining wall with a thud.

Every patron in the Valley Arms pub sat glued to the game on the huge TV screen. They groaned as one with disappointment.

"Dang it." Amy snapped her damp bar rag against the oak counter top.

"There goes our tips," Simon, her co-worker, said, his South London accent turning sour.

"Forget the tips. There goes the game," Amy said.

Loud grumbling erupted from every corner. The Valley Arms, a genuine English pub transplanted into the middle of the hot San Fernando Valley, was also the official "Atomic Center" for the LA-based soccer club. It was the hub where the Atoms' fans got together to support their team. Bright red and white banners hung from the ceiling; free snacks landed on the tables throughout the game, and half-time giveaways created a fun atmosphere. The Atoms' stadium was forty miles away, so the Valley Arms was the next best place to be if you couldn't make it to their home turf.

But not today. On the screen, Diego Torres dropped his face into his hands. He stood still for a moment while the goalie retrieved the ball. Then Torres began a slow trot back up the field, pain and disappointment etched all over his face.

"Well, there you have it, folks," the TV commentator said. "Torres's drought continues. That's his fourth shot in today's game, and not one has been on target. With a run at the play-offs coming down to the wire, Torres has to find a way to fight through this dry spell."

"You suck, Diego," a loud male voice called out from the back of the pub.

"How do you know, Fernando? You got experience with that?" another man asked.

Three burly men sitting at the table nearest the bar laughed.

"Leave him alone. Besides, there's nothing wrong with that choice." Amy shook her head as she pulled back on the tap handle and expertly shot beer into the pint glass in her hand. She came around the counter, carrying three full beers over to the guys' table.

The men all zeroed in on her chest as she set the beers down. Thanks to the ridiculous uniform with its Union Jack bra top, her breasts were front and center. She tugged at her short black jacket, but it did little to cover her curves and left her stomach completely bare. Her running joke with Simon was that, along with the short tartan skirt, the uniform looked like the bastard child of a Hooters' bar costume and a Beef Eater uniform. Simon could afford to laugh; at least his Union Jack T-shirt covered his midriff.

She deposited two beers at a table where the customers both wore the bright red Atoms jerseys. TORRES, in big, black letters, adorned the back, along with his number ten. She took the last beer to the back corner and slid it in front of Fernando.

"On the house. Drink up your sorrows and support the man. He's a great player, and when times are tough we need to stay true to our motto." She pointed to the huge banner hanging over the taps, "Atoms #1 Fans Drink Here."

"Yeah, I know, Amy. Thanks."

She patted Fernando on the shoulder and cruised back to the bar, gathering empty glasses as she went.

"Careful, Amy," Simon whispered. "Reggie said he'd fire you if you gave out any more free beers."

"Reggie's not here, is he?"

"But somehow he always knows."

"Loosen up, Si. It's good business. Fernando needs to leave here either feeling good about the game or good about the pub." She motioned to the screen where time was ticking off the clock in the top left corner. "It's not going to be the game."

The other reason that Amy had given Fernando the beer remained unspoken between them. Reggie, the English native who owned the bar, was a flat out racist. Whenever the English Premiere League was on, he was right there in the center of things, whooping and chanting as loudly as his customers. But when he had to deal with the Latino clientele that the Atoms' games invariably brought in, he couldn't keep the sneer out of his voice. He always disappeared to see to other business when the Atoms played, though he was all smiles when the Atoms' publicity people stopped by. Somehow, he had them all snowed, and the Valley Arms raked in cash for both home and away games.

Amy hated that Reggie got away with it and that she needed this job badly enough to put up with the pig.

A handsome, but balding man at the counter looked at Amy thoughtfully. "You make a good point," he said smoothly.

"About what?"

"About the relationship between happiness and financial profit. They usually walk hand in hand."

"Okay. Thanks, I guess." Amy laughed. "What can I get you?"

"What do you have?"

"We have four quality ales and Stongbow cider on tap. Fosters is our most popular. Guinness, if you like it dark. Sam Adams or Heineken if you want something familiar."

"I'll take a Fosters."

Amy moved over to the Fosters hand pump and pulled at it twice. She set the foaming glass down on the spill mat as the excess ran over. The man gingerly wrapped his fingers around the pint glass trying to get as little beer as possible on his hand.

"So you like soccer?" he asked.

Amy fixed her gaze on him. She hadn't pegged him for a talker. Frankly, sporting an expensive suit and tapping on his big-screen cellphone while the game played, he didn't fit their usual clientele profile at all. The idea that he might be from the Atoms' organization ran through her mind, but those people introduced themselves immediately. They were annoyed at having to drive out to the Valley for business, and eager to waste as little time as possible. This guy's fingernails were manicured, and he smelled of expensive cologne.

He could be hitting on her. Most men did the second they saw her skimpy top and long legs. Usually she shut them down so expertly, they didn't even see it coming. But this guy wasn't angling to get her into bed, either. It made no sense. He took a sip of his beer and looked at her expectantly for an answer.

"Do I like soccer? Yeah, I love it." Her dwindling bank account popped up in front of her face. Any talkative guy with a suit and a phone like that could throw her a tip that could make a difference, so she slid down the bar to stand right in front of him. "I played in college. Now, I'm like everyone else here. I root for the Atoms through thick and thin."

"Who's your favorite player?"

"Torres, of course."

"Good to hear. What university?"

"Sorry?"

"The university you played for?"

"One back east. The program was only so-so."

"That's because it's in the Ivy League." Simon threw the comment over his shoulder as he served another customer.

"Well, I already guessed you were smart. Which one? Harvard, Princeton..."

"No." She cut him off. Why did she suddenly feel as if she were in a job interview? "Not the big three. University of Pennsylvania. Have you heard of it?"

"Of course, Penn. Wharton School of Business, right? Donald Trump's alma matter."

"Yeah, but I was in the College of Arts and Sciences. Our alumni aren't nearly as famous, and our degrees certainly not as lucrative." She tried to take the conversation back into the land of light and breezy, the place of big tips.

The man, on the other hand, narrowed his eyes as he ran his gaze up and down her body. Not in that entitled, obvious way when men check out women standing right in front of them. But more as if she were a prize cow he was sizing up for sale at market.

"And you work here? With a degree like that?"

"I do." She shrugged as if she didn't care. "Sometimes, life just robs you of your choices. You don't have to like it, but you should make the best of it. Right?"

"Or sometimes you just need to seize the chances as they come up. If they come up. I mean, you and the chances would have to be the right fit."

"Sorry?"

"Nothing. Don't worry. I'll have to check it out. But I've got a good feeling." He nodded twice to himself and then thrust his hand over the bar counter. "I'm Paul Knight."

Amy shook off the weird vibe, and for the sake of gas in her tank that weekend clasped his hand. "Hi, I'm Amy."

"Amy who?"

"We're not allowed to give our last names out. Sorry." Simon jumped to her rescue. Not that she needed it. He stood a little too close to Amy to hit the message home.

Paul Knight opened his mouth to say something else, but the pub erupted in another loud cheer followed by even louder groan. All eyes looked to the screen on the back wall as an instant replay flashed another razor-sharp pass to Diego, who received the ball yards from the goal. A quick turn and a shot. The goalie, barely able to throw himself in front of the ball, managed to deflect it for a corner kick.

"A real chance here for Torres and the Atoms as they line up for the corner kick. That was Torres's first legitimate shot of the game. Let's see if he can capitalize on it now with the set piece. They should send the ball into him. Torres has a real ability to place the ball in the back of the net with his head. In fact, twenty percent of his goals come from headers," the announcer said.

The Valley Arms occupants watched with rapt attention.

"Come on, Diego!" Fernando called out.

Amy shot him a grin and then looked to Paul Knight. As tense as anyone in the pub, he sat straight-backed on the stool. Weird. When the Atoms were on defense, he couldn't have been less interested.

An Atoms' defender placed the ball in the corner spot, took a step back, and sent a lovely swooping cross into the center for Torres. "That could not be placed any better." The announcer built the moment. It was up to Torres to deliver. Everyone in the vicinity of the goal jumped as the ball sailed toward the center of the penalty box. Torres, flanked by two burly defenders, mistimed his jump, crashed into one, and fell in a heap to the ground.

The other defender easily pounded the ball away from the goal, and suddenly the other team was on the attack.

Torres jumped up, protesting the no-call by the referee. His face in a close-up was big and ugly on the screen as he shouted at the ref.

"He better be careful," the announcer said.

The ref turned to walk away, but Torres reached out to grab his arm.

"No! No! *No!*" Knight jumped from his stool, sending his beer sloshing over the glass.

Amy whipped around to stare at him. Suddenly, the theatrics inside the pub were as exciting as the ones on the field. She didn't know where to look. Why on earth did this man care so much?

Back on the screen, Torres tugged at the ref's shirt as he passionately continued to make his point.

"Shit!" Knight said loudly.

"Torres is in trouble here. Even youth players know you never touch the ref." The announcer's tone passed judgment on Torres and his actions.

The ref had no choice. He flashed the red card in Torres's face. The soccer player threw his arms up in disgust, yelled a few more things, and stomped off the field. He was out of the game.

The pub erupted into intense discussion, almost loud enough to drown out the announcer, who was also trying to make sense of what had just happened. "Torres is too good a player to actually think he was fouled. Something more must be going on. And so the question remains: what's wrong with Diego Torres? This is no longer just a dry spell."

Knight's eyes blazed with alarm and fury as he slammed cash on the bar. Without a word to Amy or anyone else, he strode to the door almost step for step with Torres who was marching to the locker room on the big screen. Knight banged his way out of the pub just as Torres disappeared into the stadium's tunnel.

"That was strange," Amy said to Simon, as she retrieved the paper money from the counter.

"Why do you think he cared so much?"

"Who knows. He was creepy." She fished a single coin out of the cash register. "And he only left a quarter tip." She forgot about Knight almost as soon as the coin hit the tip jar.

The game continued on the big screen as the broadcaster and his colleagues discussed Torres's meltdown. The main question being, why would a player known as the gentleman of Major League Soccer create such a scene? It interested Amy only to a point. Diego Torres's life and her own were oceans apart, and she would never sail on his starry waters.

"Hey, roomie. Can I borrow your bike?" Amy returned her car keys to the hook by the door. The gas gauge on her beat-up Civic had been hovering on empty for days. She shouldn't chance it.

"You have a shift at Starbucks?" Simon appeared in the door of his bedroom in shorts only, a guitar slung over his shoulder on a Union Jack strap. The small apartment they shared around the corner from the bar didn't have air conditioning, and during heatwaves, like the one they were having now, they wore as little as possible when they were home.

"Yes. I have two jobs, and I still can't afford to fill up my car at the gas station. So I'm doing well." Her tone was light despite her words.

"You could change that, you know." Simon shifted the guitar to his hip and fixed her with a hard gaze.

"What, get a third job?"

"No, Amy, I'm serious. That man at the pub last week was right. You're smart. You've got a head for business and a college degree. You shouldn't be frothing coffees or pulling drafts."

"You work at that same bar, you know." Amy raised her eyebrows to make the point.

"Yeah, but I have this." Simon grabbed the guitar by its neck. "It probably won't go anywhere, but at least I'm working towards something. What are you working towards?"

"Gee, I don't know, Dad. I'll have to think about that. Meanwhile, can I borrow your bike or what?"

Simon nodded, and Amy grabbed his bike lock keys from the next hook. "Thanks."

"Wait. Man U plays Liverpool tonight. Reggie wants us in an hour early."

Amy blew out a long breath. The tension of her ridiculous life burned its way through her shoulders. "Shit, yeah. I forgot. I'll be there."

"Oh, and, Ames?"

"Yes?" Her tone was perfunctory; she'd had more than enough parenting for one afternoon.

"I don't really know what I'm talking about." He looked apologetic.

"No. You do." She gave him a soft smile. "That's the problem. Si, you're my best friend, the closet thing I have to family. I should thank you for caring and not jump all over you when you do."

"Yes, you should." Simon took a step toward her, his arms stretching out for a hug.

Amy put a hand up to stop him. "I'm late. I gotta get to work."

Simon's words rattled around in her head all the way to Starbucks. True to the joke about a Starbucks on every corner, the ride wasn't far. Just long enough for the stagnant state of her life to become increasingly clear. Two crappy jobs, no relationships other than Simon, and he wanted more than she could give, even if he didn't admit it. Not long ago, she had been going places. At Penn she had been fast-tracked by eager English professors into a masters in modern British literature. She had been the darling of the department. Her parents' death and the debt they left as a parting gift had almost pulled her under. When she surfaced in LA, three thousand miles from the problem, she had jumped on the treadmill of just getting by.

She rolled into the Starbucks parking lot, depressed and preoccupied, and was startled when Paul Knight bounded out of his late-model Jaguar toward her.

"Amy Kimball, you're a hard woman to find," he called out to her.

Amy recognized him from the pub. "What the hell?" She raised the bike lock menacingly in her hand.

"No. No. It's all good." Knight stopped in his tracks. "I just got a proposition for you."

"Get away from me, you perv." She swung the bike lock in his direction.

"Not that kind of proposition. Just hear me out." He took a quick step back.

"No thanks."

"Look, I'm Paul Knight. I'm Diego Torres's manager. Get out your phone. Look me up."

Amy didn't move.

He reached into his back pocket for his billfold and pulled out a crisp one-hundred dollar bill. "I'll give you a hundred bucks if you Google me."

"So it *is* that kind of proposition."

Knight chuckled, but it wasn't a happy laugh. "The money's easier earned out here than it is in there." He tipped his head to the busy Starbucks and the line that went out the door. "You want it or not?"

He had her there. "All I gotta do is look you up?"

"Yep," he said, popping the "p" at the end of the word.

She'd be foolish not to take the money. He was buying her on some level, but what was the real difference between this and discovering a hundred bucks on the sidewalk? It was still found money. And besides, this could be the tip he hadn't given her last week. Amy slipped the bike lock between her legs, ready for a quick grab if she needed it, and pulled out her phone from her purse slung across her back.

"That's K-n-i-g-h-t," he said.

She typed his name into Safari, and up popped his picture. He and Diego Torres, standing with their arms around each other, with shit-eating grins all over their faces. She looked from her phone to the man in front of her. They were one and the same. She stepped just close enough to snatch the bill from his outstretched hand and then backed up.

"Okay, you got my attention," she said.

"Good. Because this is where it gets a little crazy."

Amy leveled a look at him. "We passed crazy five minutes ago."

"No, seriously. I do have a proposition for you. But you need to hear it at our lawyers' office, and you need to sign a confidential non-disclosure agreement before we go any further."

"This is getting too weird for me. I'm not interested." She locked the bike and moved toward the coffee house.

"Look. I'll give you five hundred bucks more. A hundred now in good faith and four hundred just for hearing me out tomorrow."

Amy skittered to a halt. Her mind vaulted over, *Careful, once he's bought you, you're done,* to six hundred dollars! *I could get new running shoes and dinner at that new up-scale Mexican restaurant, or be responsible and put gas in my tank and plunk down a couple of Benjamins on my student loans.* She turned back and looked him straight in the eye.

"How'd you find me?" she asked.

"The Internet and a good private investigator."

"That's not creepy at all."

"You're just what we're looking for." He dug another crisp bill out of his billfold and held it out for her.

"You're only proving my point here."

"Just take this now, and decide later if you want to come."

"I guess it couldn't hurt." But the alarm bells in her head rang loudly. Even though Amy didn't like the look of him or the deals he offered so slickly, she walked over and snatched the second bill out of his hand.

He grabbed a folder from his car. It had the names *Horowitz and Kane* in gold letters embossed across it.

"Here's the paperwork. This is the law firm; their address is here." He flicked it open to show her. "All my info is in there, too. The appointment's at ten in the morning." He snapped the folder shut and handed it to her. "I know you have no reason to trust me, but this is a great opportunity for you. It's only going to come around once. If you don't take it, we'll pass it on to someone else. So give it some real thought."

"Okay," Amy said through tight lips.

"Oh, and it will be much easier for you later if you don't tell anyone about this."

"That doesn't sound suspicious at all."

"You would be stupid not to think so. And we already know you're smart. If at any time you don't feel right about it, you can just walk away."

"Like right now," Amy said, turning her back on him and finally making her way into work.

CHAPTER 2

"TA." THE MANCHESTER UNITED SUPPORTER smelled of sour sweat. He thanked Amy for the pint of Guinness and doubled his thanks by slapping her behind. Her skirt was so short that he caught her cheek and cupped it for an instant.

"I'll have another one of these, duckie." He pointed to the Guinness. "And those." He pointed to her behind and then spat in his hands and rubbed them briskly together. The whole table roared with laughter.

Amy could barely choke down her disgust. That was the second time tonight. She quickly found Reggie carousing in the back with his buddies, letting Simon and Amy do all the heavy lifting, as usual.

"Your friend at table three keeps grabbing my ass." She spat the words out.

"Don't worry. It's good for business." His Manchester accent was made thicker by the four empty pint glasses in front of him.

"Well, it's not good for my ass, Reggie. And if he does it again, I'm kicking him out."

He exchanged pointed looks with the men at his table. "You can't kick anyone out of the Arms, love. It's my pub." He slid the empty glasses toward her. "Relax. It's all good fun. Clear the table, would ya?"

Amy reached out for the glasses. Her hand hovered over the first one, shaking slightly.

"They're not going to clear themselves," Reggie said.

Anger at Reggie and the state of her life boiled over. Suddenly, she knew exactly what she could buy for Knight's six hundred bucks.

"You know, Reggie, you're wrong. I can kick someone out of your pub." She tipped the glass over so the dregs ran out. "Me! I quit!"

She would have given anything to storm out, slamming the door behind her. But those kind of dramatics only worked in the movies. Aware that everyone's eyes were now on her, she grabbed her purse from behind the bar with a flourish and downed a quick shot of Reggie's best Scotch. The alcohol burned her throat on the way down, but its warmth hit her immediately.

This is what freedom must feel like.

Simon stood before her open-mouthed. She gave him a quick squeeze on his arm, and had her hand on the door when Reggie's voice boomed out, "Oi! That uniform's not yours, missy!"

She stopped in her tracks, her back to him and the entire, expectant pub. Then the devil took her. With a simple shrug the black jacket fell to

19

the floor. The Union Jack bra top was another matter, though. She shimmied and twisted, trying to get it over her head without looking foolish. Finally, with one arm over her naked front, she flung the bra top over her shoulder back into pub.

The place erupted with cheers.

"Take it all off!" someone shouted.

"You wish." Her heart pounding with excitement and embarrassment, Amy pushed through the door. "Sleep tight, ya morons!"

Outside the warm night air hit her like a tonic. Her shoulders dropped what felt like a foot, and for the first time in ages the deep breath she sucked in actually made it to the bottom of her lungs. Walking out of the back door of the Valley Arms free and clear was the best thing that had happened to her in a long while. She even managed to hold her head high and her arm around her chest as she passed two men getting out of a car. They whistled appreciatively as she passed, and she was thankful that she still had the tartan skirt on. A symbolic gesture only went so far.

Her high only lasted until she slipped the Atoms promotional shirt, conveniently sitting on the backseat of her car, over her head. Once fully clothed she took stock of her situation. Despite her victorious exit, it wasn't good. Reggie was a racist, misogynistic asshole, and probably a hundred other horrible things as well, but he was the devil she knew. Now, if she wanted to eat, she would have to metaphorically get into bed with Paul Knight, the devil she didn't know. And do it tomorrow morning at 10 a.m. exactly. Anxiety curled in whips in her stomach. What exactly had she gotten herself into?

The appointment was on her before she knew it. She had gotten up early to run before it got too hot, and to work off the nervous energy that was now coursing through her body. At the end of the run, she stopped by Blinkies, Simon's favorite donut shop, for two of the apple fritters he loved. She owed him big for dumping a ton of extra work on him with her dramatic exit. She didn't want to talk, though, so she sneaked in and left a note with the fritters on the kitchen counter, then jumped into the shower. At 9:20 a.m., she made her escape, and by 9:55 a.m., she stood in her one good dress—its straps cutting into her shoulders—in the shining lobby of the Horowitz and Kane law firm.

The receptionist tossed her thick blonde curls out her of eyes as she got up to take Amy to Franklin Horowitz's office.

Amy was sure that the casual motion had been perfected in front of a mirror since it simultaneously thrust the receptionist's large breasts forward. She might have enjoyed the show if her stomach wasn't turning cartwheels.

"My name's Jenna," the receptionist said, as they walked toward the elevator. "Please let me know if there's anything else I can help you with."

The elevator doors opened several floors up. Jenna passed Amy on to Horowitz's personal secretary, Rachel, a thin, crisp lady who stood waiting for them in a bright outer office.

"We've been expecting you, Ms. Kimball. Come with me, please." There was no tossing of hair or thrusting of breasts on the rarefied atmosphere of the top floor. Rachel escorted Amy to a corner office suite.

Behind the glass doors, Paul Knight lolled on a couch, and a thick-set man in a very expensive suit sat behind a huge desk; both were waiting on her arrival.

Amy took a look at the exit. This was her last chance to bail. So far everything seemed on the up and up. Rachel tapped on the glass door and opened it. After taking a deep breath, Amy strode through.

Knight bounced up from the gray plush couch and rushed to meet her. "Amy, so good to see you. I wasn't sure you'd make it."

"Neither was I," she said, and took his outstretched hand. His shake was firm, but his hands were much too soft. And there was that weird vibe with him again.

"This is Franklin Horowitz," he said.

They shook hands, and she was directed to a chair that matched the couches. She sank into it, and her eyes widened. It was by far the most comfortable thing she had ever sat on. She ran her hand over the soft fabric, then sat up straight to gather her wits about her; she couldn't be seduced by the first piece of flashy furniture to come her way.

"I'm sure you're wondering why you're here," Horowitz said. His voice was smooth and deep and very reassuring.

"It did cross my mind."

"Before we get to that, you need to sign this." He handed her a contract that had *Confidentiality Agreement* in big bold letters written across the top of the first page.

She flipped through the rest to see a long list of numbers with several bullet points after each one. "I would like to read it first."

"Of course," Horowitz said. "Can Rachel get you anything while you do so?"

"A coffee, please."

Rachel came back in to offer a choice between a regular coffee, a latte, or a cappuccino.

Amy asked for a latte and for half a second savored being the costumer and not the barista. She turned her attention to the contract in her hands. One pre-law class at Penn was not enough for her to truly comprehend what she was reading, but she read every word and underlined key phrases with her finger. Basically the agreement said that the three of them would have a conversation, and subsequently, she could not let a word or even an inference leave this room. If she did, all sorts of terrible things would happen, not the least of which would be lawsuits, court cases, and debt up to her eyeballs. In short, her life would be over.

Rachel returned with a latte, which she placed before her on a Horowitz and Kane coaster. Amy took one sip and knew that the coffee was a South American blend and that the firm had a very expensive coffee machine. The fact that she knew more about the latte than her reading material sent her back to the contract with a renewed focus.

She finished reading and paused, her pen hovering over the line with her name printed under it. She resisted the urge to run her fingers through her hair. Should she sign? Should she just get up and walk out? The remaining four hundred dollars had appeared at the other end of the coffee table while she read. It was a clear draw, but what finally put her over the edge was simple curiosity. There was no way that she could live the rest of her life not knowing what all this was about. Probably the conversation would be a huge disappointment. She might very well end up behind bars, but at least she would know.

She signed. The expensive pen moved smoothly over the thick paper.

Paul Knight licked his lips as if he were about to devour something very tasty. Horowitz picked up the money and handed it to her in a slick trade for the contract. "Okay. Down to business. Rachel, can you step in here one last time. Ms. Kimball, just to make sure that you're on the up and up, we would like Rachel to pat you down to make sure that you're not wearing a recording device."

"Are you kidding me?" When he didn't react, she said. "I just signed the agreement."

"You can never be too careful."

Amy stretched her arms out as an answer. Rachel patted her down without making eye contact. "Nothing there." She nodded at Horowitz.

Amy wondered if patting down women was in her job description. She raised an eyebrow and tilted her head at the men. "Well?"

"Remember, what we're about to tell you is completely confidential," Knight began. Amy nodded for the umpteenth time.

Knight thrust his head forward. "We want to offer you a job. It pays very well. Fifteen hundred dollars a week plus room and board."

Amy couldn't believe her ears. They knew how to get a girl's attention, all right.

"Doing what?" she asked. Her mind was already whirling into high gear. She could do a lot with that kind of money, like get new running shoes and pay off student loans and maybe even make a dent in the debt her parents left.

"We want you to date one of our clients," Paul Knight stated.

Her stomach dropped, and a slow flush crept up her throat into her cheeks. "Christ. I'm a bartender, not a prostitute."

"Nobody said you were," Horowitz jumped in, raising a palm to Knight who was already opening his mouth. "You're going about this all wrong, Paul. Sit down. Let me do the talking."

Knight's jaw jutted, but he sat down and shut up.

"We have a client. A famous client, who, shall we say, has certain proclivities that if they were to come to light would destroy his career. Not his main career, you understand, but the only one that matters. His endorsement deals are worth multi-millions. We want to protect those deals by creating a diversion, and you would be that diversion."

"What are the proclivities? I'm not getting involved with drugs or anything illegal."

"No. It's nothing like that," Horowitz said. "Our client prefers the company of men."

"He's gay?" Amy asked.

"Yes," Knight said, and looked as if the admission had personally wounded him.

Amy's mind whirled, putting the puzzle pieces together as fast as she could. "How's that a problem? This is LA, after all. And Diego Torres would be the second person to come out in the league this year. What's the big deal?" She took a calculated risk by naming Torres. Of course, she didn't know for sure that the conversation was about him, but Knight was his manager and concern over these "certain proclivities" going public would go a long way to explain what was troubling his game lately. More important, if she was right, she might get a leg up on these men and this situation.

"I told you she was smart," Knight threw at Horowitz.

"No matter. It's better to have it all out in the open." Horowitz focused all his attention back on Amy. "But you couldn't be more wrong, Ms. Kimball. If Torres came out, it would be a very big deal. So big, it might ruin his entire career. Most people aren't as liberal as the ones in this office."

"Is Torres with someone? Is that why you guys are so worried?" Amy asked.

"No. He says there's no one," Knight said, "Just the fear of being found out is killing Diego and his game."

"To put it in simple terms, Ms. Kimball," Horowitz said, "we would like to pay you real money to have a fake relationship with Diego Torres."

"So you need a beard. Torres and I would date?" She settled deeper into the chair. The possibility was intriguing. Tell a little lie here and there. The money was great, and it might even be fun, and best of all, she wouldn't have to go crawling back to Reggie. "Why me?"

"You met all the criteria when we did the background search," Knight said. "You're smart. You graduated summa cum laude from an Ivy League School. I saw you in action at the Valley bar, so I know it's not just academic smarts. You played soccer at a competitive level at Penn, and you were a starter every year, except for your junior year out in London where, I believe, you played on a coed team for King's College?"

Amy nodded. They had clearly done all their homework.

"You have no family to question whatever you do next," Knight continued. "And you don't seem to have had any relationships, long-term or otherwise, that could compromise you now."

Their first misstep. But how could they know about Darla? She should tell them that she was into girls. Full disclosure and all.

"And I'm broke," she said instead.

"Yes, I guess that's the most important factor for you," Horowitz said. "And a major bargaining chip for us. We're willing to make this worth your while, Ms. Kimball."

"Okay. So we would go to dinner and movies and make appearances together?"

"No. We want to completely squash this thing before any rumors start escaping. So we would need more of a commitment from you."

"Like what?"

"There would be dating, of course, but we need you to move into his house within a few weeks. You would have to get engaged."

"Engaged? In a few weeks? No one's gonna buy that. You might as well sew a rainbow flag onto his uniform."

Horowitz suppressed a laugh, which was not the reaction Amy was expecting. "We have a fake relationship already in place. If you agree, you have been secretly dating Diego for months. He loves you desperately, but it's a Romeo and Juliet kind of thing. His family wants him to marry a Latina and a Catholic. So keeping this kind of secret from his family has been tearing him apart. On and off the field."

A thousand questions flew into Amy's mind. "And Torres is completely on board with all this? He doesn't want to meet me first?"

"We'll get to that. But you're his type. If he had this kind of type," Knight said, but he wouldn't meet Amy's gaze. "Let's just say, he understands the severity of the situation. All Diego needs to do is look like a movie star and produce on the field. We take care of the rest. That's what he pays us for. And that's why we're prepared to pay you very handsomely, too."

Amy gave him her best withering gaze.

"He's met you on paper," Horowitz added. "He likes what he's seen."

"Well, I would have to meet him in person first. And if I like him, how long would this contract last? We wouldn't actually get married, would we?"

"We would contract you to six months, and no, you wouldn't actually get married. But we do reserve the right to renegotiate as we go along." Horowitz smoothed a non-existent wrinkle on his sleeve.

"Of course you do." Amy bit her bottom lip.

"Not to flatter you into a decision here, Ms. Kimball. But we have been looking for some time now. We're convinced that we have finally found the right person." Horowitz retrieved another set of papers from his desk. He held them out to Amy. "So what do you say? This is a great opportunity for someone in your position. Are you ready to sign the real contract?"

That was the million-dollar question. She should just get up and walk out of the office without looking back and leave the contract on the table. But what was she walking out to? Wasn't something better than nothing at all? Her mind ran through the potential outcomes, but what it really came down to was whether to jump off this particular precipice or not. The jump wouldn't kill her. But the landing might, and that was the real problem.

"Can I think about it?"

"You can, but this offer expires at six tonight. Sharp." Horowitz returned the papers to his desk. His expression, so eager and friendly before, had hardened.

"Gone like it never existed." Knight waved his hand through the air as if he were performing a magic trick. "Face it. You only get one shot at this fairy tale. And the castle doors are closing fast."

"So until you sign, I believe our business is concluded." Horowitz pushed a button on his desk.

Rachel appeared at Amy's side. "I'll see you out, Ms. Kimball."

Without a signed contract, Amy lost what little leverage she had in that room. Horowitz sat at his desk, already lost to his computer screen. Knight whipped out his phone to check his messages. Rachel directed her through the double glass doors with a grip of steel. The outer office seemed noisier now. Everyone had a reason to be here, a purpose to their day, except her. Rachel hurried her toward the elevators where Jenna stood waiting.

"Good day, Ms. Kimball." Rachel handed her over.

"Hey." Jenna smiled the moment Rachel turned her back. "Did it go well?"

"Not sure yet."

"Well, they're really good here. They've lots of famous clients. You never know who you'll meet."

Amy realized Jenna assumed she was interviewing for a job. In a way, she was.

Jenna hit the elevator button and leaned in close. "That's Kevin Wilson over there," she whispered, and pointed to another glass-walled office. "He does all his business here. See? That's how good they are."

Amy had heard of Kevin Wilson, the lead guitarist for Krippled Kids. Who hadn't? Before she turned her head to gawk, she took a quick peek down Jenna's top. She couldn't help herself. Jenna threw her breasts around like an engraved invitation. They were large and firm and maybe even real, and were well worth the shame that flitted through Amy at peeking. At some point, she would have to get back on the romance wagon, but for now she was content to run alongside of it.

"Oh! I think they closed a deal." Jenna's breasts jiggled with excitement.

Amy forced her gaze toward the office.

Kevin Wilson, in jeans and a black T-shirt emblazoned with his own face, high-fived a man in a tailored suit.

"What kind of deal?" Amy asked.

"I don't know. Record deal, maybe. Our entertainment law division is very active."

"Really? You have an entertainment division?" Amy tilted her head and considered the scene before her. The man in the suit was now patting Kevin Wilson on the shoulder and grinning from ear to ear. Clearly they were both very happy.

The elevator dinged its arrival, and Jenna held the door back while Amy entered.

"Yes, that's why I have to escort you in and out until you get this." Jenna flashed her employee badge at her hip. "We take our clients' privacy very seriously. You never know who's around."

"Afraid I'm gonna run over for an autograph?"

"You never know."

Jenna stood too close in the elevator. Amy focused on the descending floor numbers above the door. It was too easy to succumb and cop another look down Jenna's top, but she withheld. She had been on the receiving end of the same stares too often at the Valley Arms; it felt cheap doing the same thing to Jenna.

In the lobby, she said her good-byes and went over to the bench seats on the far side of the entrance. She turned on her phone. Simon had texted her about a million times wanting to know where she was and if she was okay. She swiped the messages off her screen; she would deal with Simon later. In an instant, she brought up Paul Knight's info. Her thumbs froze over the keyboard as she rocked gently back and forth, considering her next move very carefully.

She needed to take her own advice. There was no way to know if jumping, metaphorically, into bed with Torres was a bad or good idea until the six months were officially over. She could roll the pros and cons around in her head until 5:59 p.m., and still she wouldn't know one way or the other. All she had to do right now was decide if she was going to jump at all. And why not? She didn't have a job, or any money. She had to find a way to move forward.

Her thumbs flew over the keyboard. *I'm in. With one condition. Non-negotiable.*

If she liked Torres enough to sign on, she would get a music contract for Simon, and hope against hope, that one unselfish act would buy her enough karma for that safe landing.

CHAPTER 3

Amy's Civic putted loudly into Knight's driveway. She killed the engine and puffed a sigh of relief. The temperature gauge had hovered right below the big H all the way up the hill. She hadn't been sure she would make it. Knight lived on the mountain crest that separated the Valley from the trendy Westside. The sleek lines of his house gleamed in the sunlight. It must have cost a pretty penny. No wonder he was so anxious to get this party started. Diego wasn't the only one in jeopardy here, Amy realized. A lot of fancy incomes rode on this plan working.

Knight opened the door before she could ring the bell. He ushered her into his living room where Diego Torres, as breathtakingly handsome as his billboard posters, stood in the middle of the room holding a bouquet of white roses. His handsome, chiseled features were softened by warm, brown eyes, and his crisp linen suit enhanced the athletic body underneath.

Amy felt shoddy, dressed in the same casual sun dress she had worn to Horowitz's office only a few days before. It was the nicest dress she had, and she knew it highlighted her long legs, but still, she'd need to acquire a whole new wardrobe for this gig. "Hi. I'm Amy. You must be Diego?"

"Pleased to meet you." His slight accent made his voice almost musical. "These are for you." He held out the roses.

"I told Diego he didn't have to bring a bouquet. This isn't a real date," Knight said.

"Yes, we know, Paul. But any fake relationship that starts with flowers has a chance to turn into real friendship." Diego flashed his thousand-watt smile.

Amy was dazzled—not by his star power, although she could see its draw, but more by what was underneath the smile, a slight twitch at the edge of his bottom lip. Diego was as nervous as she was.

"Thank you," she said, taking the bouquet. "White roses are my favorite."

"I know. It was in the file Paul gave me."

"Was it? I don't remember that." Paul shrugged.

Amy found the idea of a dossier creepy, but the fact that Diego had studied it felt sweet. Diego shuffled on his feet. Unlike Knight, he knew that this thing could go either way. His unease tugged at her. "They're lovely." She tried to put him at ease.

Diego motioned to the couches. Knight grabbed a tray of sparkling water and fruit kebabs from the kitchen.

"I don't eat anything with added sugar during the season," Diego said apologetically as Knight set the tray on the coffee table.

"No, these look great." Mangoes and fresh coconut were the kind of fruit she and Simon couldn't normally afford. "Paul, did you put these together?" She stifled a laugh as she imagined him in an apron sliding the fruit onto the sticks.

"No," Diego said, "They are from a fruit cart from my old neighborhood. I was out there visiting my parents. Normally they would come with chili powder and lime, but I thought you might want to ease into my native cuisine slowly." He smiled.

"That actually sounds really good."

Diego smiled again, this time without the twitch. Knight made a happy clucking noise from his chair.

They started talking about Mexican cuisine, and Amy found she was genuinely interested in the conversation. She also learned that Diego had a wry sense of humor as well as a natural humbleness about his athletic ability and movie-star looks. Much to her surprise, she actually liked him.

Toward the end of the meeting, Diego leaned toward her. "I know this whole thing is... unconventional, to say the least," he said. "But I'm in a real bind, and you're perfect. I hope you can see your way to help me." Diego addressed her like an equal, and suddenly the business proposal that had seemed seedy became a compliment, all wrapped up in a personal favor to him. "Do you think you could?" he asked.

Amy gave him a soft smile. "I think I'd like to try."

TOP STORY: Internet Edition

SOCCER HEARTTHROB! SERIOUS SECRET GIRLFRIEND!
By Diane Garza

Diego Torres, of the LA Atoms has been keeping a secret, and it's a BIGGY.

Torres introduced his twenty-five-year-old girlfriend, Amy Kimball, via social media Friday, sharing a selfie of the happy couple at the Atoms' training facility. The couple met at a publicity event in Calabasas, California, in the spring and have been hot and heavy ever since.

"She's everything I've always dreamed of," the hunky soccer star captioned the photo.

Sources close to Torres claim that he had been keeping the relationship under wraps in deference to his ninety-

three year-old great-grandmother, who begged him to date within his culture and faith. Kimball is neither Latina nor Catholic. Keeping this secret from his loved ones has taken its toll on Torres on the field, who has not scored in the last five games.

When asked about the relationship, Kimball, a soccer player in her own right, joked, "We're having a ball."

STAY INFORMED?
Sign up for our newsletter and other special offers.

"Wanna tell me what this is all about?" Simon stood before her in nothing but his shorts in the hot and airless apartment. He thrust his cell phone in her face.

Garza's news item was splashed all over the screen. Diego had taken the selfie, his free arm wrapped around Amy, who was snuggled into him, laughing at whatever he was saying. They looked like a happy, natural couple, and very much in love.

"Oh my God. Is it up?" Amy snatched the phone and examined the flattering photo. Her easy smile popped out from the screen. She looked fun and approachable. Her freshly washed hair fell in waves, and the bags under her green eyes were gone since she was finally sleeping these last few nights rather than working shifts. Though she wouldn't put it past Paul Knight to have had them airbrushed out. It was the most perfect, supposedly spontaneous, photo to introduce her and Diego to the world. Knight had rejected about a hundred other supposedly spontaneous moments. No question about it, he was good at his job, like most control freaks.

"So you know about this?" Simon ran a hand over his close-cropped hair and fixed her with a narrow-eyed gaze.

Amy hoped it was because he was hot rather than upset with her. "Of course I do. He's my... boyfriend." She tried to infuse happiness into the word, but it just came off as smug. Her stomach dropped when she saw the hurt in Simon's eyes.

"Really? You never told me." He reached for his phone and immediately cleared the screen.

"I couldn't tell anyone." She had begged Knight to be able to ease Simon into her new reality before the story came out, but he hadn't wanted to risk a leak. She had caved to his demands, partly because she had been dreading this exact moment. Now, she struggled for a way out, whishing she hadn't been such a coward. "Diego wanted to tell his family first." The lie rolled thickly off her tongue, but she managed to push it out. She'd known this moment would be hard but not this hard.

"Ames, this doesn't make any sense."

"How so?"

"Well, for starters, when did you have time to have this relationship no one knew about?"

"Um... I wasn't really sick a couple of weeks ago." She marveled that it took another lie to tell the "truth" and that there was no shallow end to the pool she was now floundering in. What a mess. The last thing she had wanted to do was hurt Simon.

"Your head cold was fake? That was some good acting." Simon considered her carefully, shifting from one foot to the other.

"And I actually quit Starbucks weeks ago. I'm sorry, Simon. I had to keep it a secret."

Simon opened his mouth, closed it, and then opened it again. "I always kind of thought you were gay?"

Me too. Amy pursed her lips. "No," she said softly.

"I mean, if you really liked guys..." He shook his head and started again. "I would have... I... Things might have been different."

Amy knew what he meant. But it had always been a non-starter. Even so, she clenched her jaw so the truth wouldn't spill out. She was bursting to tell him that no matter how crazy all it seemed, she hadn't forgotten about him. That he had to trust her and things would be better for both of them. That he shouldn't worry because she had it all under control.

But did she, really? Diego was a great guy and all, but had she signed away her integrity with a Mont Blanc pen? Silence fell between them.

"You're really going with this crazy story?" Simon asked. Clearly he didn't buy any part of it. "Ames, we tell each other everything. Are you sure there's nothing else you want to tell me?"

There was. A million things. Like since the moment she had left Horowitz's office with the final contract signed, she breathed a little easier. Or that she slept through the night now that her bank account was no longer hovering around zero, or that not having to endure Reggie and all his crap at the Valley Arms had freed her soul.

Amy wanted to mix up a batch of margaritas with her best friend, knock back a few, and then laugh as they threw ice cubes at each other in the sweltering heat. Mostly she wanted to tell him that she taken his advice to move forward, and that above all she didn't want to lose him. Instead, she said, "Yes. You should know that I'm moving in with the guy."

"What?" Simon's response was choked.

"He's worried about the publicity and everything, and he thinks I'll be safer if I'm with him." Amy rushed through the explanation. There was no getting out of this well, so she decided on getting out of it fast.

"Wow." Simon took a step back, the hurt in his eyes spreading to his whole face.

Amy shrugged as if it was no big deal; another action she instantly regretted. She fumbled trying to make it better. "Don't worry. I'll still pay my half of the rent. Until you can find another roommate and all."

Simon's expression hardened.

Amy bit her lip. Another terrible misstep. Why hadn't she prepared for this better?

Simon shook his head at her. "Good. Because that was my only real concern." His sarcasm rolled at her in waves. "I'm not sure what you're up to, Amy, but I hope you're being smart about it." He turned toward his room. The door made a soft pop as he closed it. Amy wished he had slammed it on her. It was what she deserved.

"Me too," she told the empty room.

Two days later, Knight pulled up in his gorgeous blue Jag to take her to Diego's house. Simon was nowhere to be seen. Amy said her good-byes to him in a note. It said, *See you soon.*

Amy silently stared out the passenger side window for the twenty-minute drive. She slid her finger down the window and traced a small S.

"What's the matter?" Knight finally asked.

"Nothing." Knight was the last person she wanted to share any of her personal feelings with.

"You better get your game face on, princess. You'll need to hit the ground running as soon as we get there," Knight said. "Diego may be out of town, but everyone else will be there. You remember their names and what they do, yeah?" He fiddled with his phone.

Amy turned to face him. She would figure out how to fix all this with Simon later.

"Yeah." She had received a folder two days ago to memorize and then destroy. It held little bits and pieces any girl should know about her boyfriend. Trivial things, like his favorite color, the members of his family, his favorite foods, and the names of Diego's house staff. Luckily, Amy had always been a quick study, and the mundane facts were easily stored away at the back of her mind.

"We're just about to get on the plane. What's up, Paul?" Diego's voice suddenly echoed on the car's Bluetooth. Knight must have called him.

"You're on speaker phone. I'm driving Amy over to your house," Knight said.

"That's good news. Hola, Amy."

"Hi, Diego."

"We won. I scored."

"I know. Congrats."

"We're just about to board. We can celebrate everything when—"

"Look," Knight jumped in. "There's not much time here, and I just wanted you to reconsider the whole sleeping arrangement thing."

"For the last time, a good Catholic boy would not move his girlfriend, or even his fiancée, into his bedroom before marriage."

"Maybe, if this was for real. But we want the public to think you're banging this girl."

Amy cringed. When had Knight turned into Reggie with better clothes? "Going too far with this pretense is worse than not going far enough. Think what's on the line here," Knight continued.

Diego's voice turned steely. "Paul, I don't want to discuss this again. I told you this is not up for negotiation. I need my privacy, and so does Amy. I want to go on record that we're saving ourselves for marriage. Right, Amy?"

"Right." Amy answered.

"Diego—" Knight started.

"Not negotiating this."

"Okay..." Knight tapped his fingers on the steering wheel. "I might be able to spin the good Catholic boy bit. It might even get us more endorsements."

Amy rolled her eyes; this guy was a machine.

"I'm hanging up now. See you later, Amy." The line went dead.

"Here." Knight tossed a square ring box onto her lap.

"What's this?"

"Your engagement ring."

"When did we become engaged? I thought we were waiting?"

"Change of plans. We ran it through a super-secret focus group, and they thought the time was right."

"Do I get a say in any of this?" Amy snapped open the box. A large diamond solitaire winked up at her.

"It's not real, but it's good quality. No one should be able to tell the difference. Put it on."

Amy slid the ring on. It fit a little snugly, but then this whole situation was starting to feel a little too tight.

"Let me give you some constructive criticism. I don't know what's going on with you right now, but you need to act happy," Knight said. "You're moving in with your fiancé and you've got a huge diamond ring to show off. You're like a princess living a real fairy tale. Once we get there, that's the face people want to see. Not some mope."

"Got it." And she did. She had signed the contract. Knight and Horowitz were going to get their money's worth. As soon as the Jag came to a stop outside Diego's mansion, Amy bounced out of the car with a smile a mile wide. She took in her surroundings with an awe and enthusiasm that became more genuine the more she saw.

Diego lived in the gated community of Hidden Hills in the north-west end of the Valley. The top-notch security was the main draw for the celebrities and sports stars who lived there.

Diego's house was in the southwest Spanish colonial-style with a terracotta-tiled roof and cream-colored stucco walls covered with bright bougainvillea blossoms. It looked elegant and graceful and at the same time welcoming. A middle-aged couple stood in the shade of the veranda. The man raised his hand casually as soon as Amy emerged from the Jag. The woman had unnaturally red hair that clashed with her purple polo shirt; she stepped forward, her hand outstretched.

"Hi. I'm Tammy," she said, her voice gravelly and harsh. She pumped Amy's hand hard. Her gaze raked across Amy, sizing her up. "My. Ain't you a pretty one, sweetie."

Amy's hackles rose. The undercurrent that thrummed from Tammy warned her to keep an eye on this one. According to the information Knight had sent over, Tom and Tammy Winters were live-ins who had joined Diego's household when he landed the Adidas advertising contract that had transformed his life.

"Thank you. I'm thrilled to be here," she said.

"This is my husband, Tom," Tammy said.

Tom stepped forward, his hand also outstretched. He beamed at her, and his smile, unlike his wife's, ran all the way to his eyes. "I'll get your bags."

"I can do that." Amy started to move back to the car.

Knight popped open the trunk and stood looking at her bags as if they were garbage sacks.

Tammy linked Amy's arm and pulled her away. "Let the men sort it out. I'll show you the estate and the apartment where you'll be staying."

On the surface the statement was friendly enough, but Amy heard an undertone saying, this is my house and you're the guest. She played her part and nodded eagerly.

The estate, as Tammy called it, was spectacular. She wouldn't have been at all surprised if hidden trumpets played a little fanfare as the carved, ornate oak door slowly opened before her. The foyer was breathtaking. Mexican tile ran the length of the room which led to a step-down living area on one side and a wrought iron staircase on the other. A huge vase overflowing with colorful birds of paradise flowers sat on the hall table. Delightful, cool air hit her as soon as she walked in. Her days of sweltering in sport tops and shorts during a heatwave were over. Guilt at leaving Simon to suffer alone shot through her, but she pushed it away.

A soft click-clack came down the hallway, and a little black and white mutt skidded toward her on the tiles.

"Oh my God, is that Dulce?"

Tammy nodded.

"Diego said she was cute, but not the cutest thing ever!" For the first time her role seemed almost natural.

"The name suits her. She's a very sweet dog," Tammy said.

As if to prove the point, Dulce climbed up Amy's leg, and she immediately lifted the dog into her arms. One touch of the soft fur and Amy fell in love for real. It seemed to work both ways. When Amy placed Dulce back on the floor the dog licked her bare ankle and nestled between her feet.

"Diego asked me to show you to your room as soon as you got here. He fixed it up himself." Tammy led the way into the back of the house. Amy followed with Dulce at her heels.

My room. She looked at her watch. She wanted to mark the first time when Knight hadn't gotten his own way.

Tammy trotted up the rear stairway that came off from the huge eat-in kitchen. They entered a hallway and on to a beautiful one bedroom apartment. A furnished living room flowed through to a small, but well-appointed kitchenette. The bedroom was ensuite and completed the living space. Diego's touch, she gathered, were the white roses everywhere.

"Oh my God. This is unbelievable." Amy bent over the vase on the breakfast bar and smelled the roses. "These are my favorites, you know."

"Yes, Diego told me."

"He did all this for me?"

"Well, the apartment was already here. He designed it for his great-grandmother when he built the gym underneath, but she preferred to stay with her granddaughter instead. So she gave up all this. Can you believe it?" Clearly Tammy didn't approve.

Amy spun around. She had never lived anywhere so lovely. With perks like this her lies would be easier to tell, making the slippery slope even deadlier. Already she was being seduced. Definitely not a good thing.

The tour continued. Tammy pointed out the apartment over the garage where she and Tom lived. Upstairs, in Amy's wing, there were another four guest bedrooms. Diego's suite was more private and tucked away on the far side of the hacienda. Tammy didn't show her; instead, she waved her hand vaguely toward the rear of the house. They came back through the kitchen and out onto the lush grounds.

The outdoor living space was an entertainment paradise. A huge pool, along with a Jacuzzi, dominated the outdoor space. The main feature was a waterfall cut into a rocky outcrop that supplied a constant cascade of crystal water that sounded beautiful. To the left stood a shaded gallery housing an outdoor kitchen with eating area, and across from that was a sunken fire-pit for stargazing on clear desert nights.

"You can lie in the pool in the summer and watch a movie on the screen that pops down from here." Tammy pointed to a box in the roof.

"No way."

"I know. You've really hit the jackpot," she said pointedly, and then indicated a pool house at the far end of the property. "That's the office. Casey can help you with scheduling and arrangements.

If you want to do anything with Diego you need to run it by Casey first."

"Okay." *Damn. Who was Casey?* Amy recalled the staff bios. *Oh, yes, the PA!* She hoped he was a little easier to read than Tammy.

Paul Knight pushed the patio doors open and stepped across the pink flagstones to Amy's side. They both stood at the pool's edge. He waved his hand theatrically. "Pretty nice spread, huh."

"You're telling me. You know that there's a screen that pulls down and you can watch movies in the pool?"

"Yes." Knight patted her shoulder patronizingly. "I know. So you're good?" He looked at his watch as if he were late for a most pressing appointment.

"Yes. I'm good. I can take it from here."

"Yes, she needs time to settle in." Tammy grasped Knight by the arm and led him back to the house.

Finally, Amy was alone. Little waves of anxiety lapped at her. So much could go wrong. What if no one actually bought the charade that she and Diego were a couple? What if she couldn't pull it off? Amy hadn't seriously considered the fallout if it all blew up in her face. She had already hurt Simon, one of the nicest guys in the world. Now she was meeting the people central to Diego's life. Paul Knight was wrong. These people would never fall for a cheap trick like this. She was a phony, a cliché who'd sold her soul for a huge paycheck.

Just as the negative thoughts began to overpower her, Dulce trotted up. Her gentle, dark eyes made Amy's heart melt. She stooped, picked up the little dog, and buried her face into Dulce's soft coat.

"It's going to be okay, right, Dulce?" Her voice was muffled against the fur.

"Sorry?" The modulated female voice came from directly behind her.

Amy swung round startled, and Dulce leaped from her arms to run to the stranger. Amy lost her balance, and teetered at the edge of the pool. Her arms flailed out trying to regain her step.

"Careful. Careful!" The woman stepped forward, reaching for her.

Amy grabbed for the proffered hand and missed. Instead, she snagged a handful of T-shirt. They both spun on their heels, teetering in the danger zone.

Dulce yipped frantically.

"My computer!" the woman cried, and in a precision move only a few could have pulled off, simultaneously grabbed Amy and swung her backward onto the tiles. A computer bag was flung at her, catching her in the gut, but she hung on to it. The bag's owner spiraled gracefully into the pool with a loud splash.

Amy lay on the flagstones, mouth agape, the wind knocked out of her. "Oh my God. Are you okay?" She leaped up, ignoring the stabbing pain in her hip.

Dulce, barking non-stop, raced along the pool's edge.

The woman bobbed to the surface and started treading water. "Son of a bitch." She glared at Amy. "Dulce, please. No barking."

Dulce whimpered, but did as she was told.

Who was she? "I'm so very sorry." Amy reached out. "Here. Let me help you."

"No, thanks."

Amy flushed at the rejection and instead watched the woman swim toward the pool ladder with slow, easy strokes, and heave herself out. Water poured off of her and the flagstones at her feet turned a deeper shade of rose. Her T-shirt clung to her like a second skin revealing a lean body with high firm breasts. The cotton pants hugged long, muscular legs. Amy tried not to stare, but there was something about the woman that invited it. She stood confident, if sopping wet, and still somehow seemed to be totally in control. A tingle ran through Amy's stomach and settled in her groin.

The woman ran a hand through her short blonde hair and then shook it. Drops of water flew across the patio and Dulce chased the light spray.

"I really am sorry." Amy moved toward her only to be pulled up by an icy stare that was not at all welcoming.

"My computer. Did it make it?"

"Yes." Amy handed it over. "Alive and well. That was some move. The spin and throwing the computer bag at me thing." Amy fell into her easy way that usually won people over in a heartbeat.

"Well, it worked out for you." The woman wrung out her T-shirt. The action pulled the shirt even tighter over her breasts. "Me, not so much."

Amy forced herself to look away. Her only hope was that despite knowing Dulce's name, she was not an integral part of the household. She was going to have trouble keeping her loving eyes on Diego if all she wanted to do was stare at this woman's chest.

The whooshing noise of the sliding glass patio door brought Tammy to their side. She had a towel in her hands and threw it over the woman's shoulders. "Casey! What happened?"

"Oh my God. You're Casey? I thought you were a man." Amy blurted the words out before she thought about them. She cursed Paul Knight and his paper-thin intel.

"Then you need a lesson in anatomy," Casey said, as she rubbed the towel through her hair giving herself an attractive tousled look. "Thanks, Tammy."

"Sorry, but when Diego mentioned his assistant, Casey, somehow your gender never came up."

Casey cast a questioning look to Tammy as if to ask, who the hell is this idiot?

"I see you have met Amy." Tammy answered the unspoken question.

Casey stiffened. "You're Amy?" She glared at her as if she couldn't believe it.

"Yeah. Please, forgive me. This is not the way I wanted to meet—"

"No worries." Her tone was light, but her eyes had frozen to a glacial blue. "If you'll excuse me. I need to get out of these wet things." She slung the precious computer bag over her shoulder, smiled thinly at Tammy, and headed off with squishy steps to the pool house at the far end of the courtyard.

Amy watched the trail of Casey's wet footprints as if they were magical. "Great. That was a terrible first impression."

"Don't worry too much about it. She's a tough nut to crack."

Was Tammy trying to make her feel better?

"All you have to know about Casey," Tammy said, "is that she is devoted to Diego. As we all are, if you get my meaning." The veiled threat came through loud and clear. Tammy leveled her gaze at Amy. "No one here wants to see him hurt."

"I don't plan on hurting him," Amy said, suddenly on the defensive. If anything this game would hurt her.

"Good. Because, you see, we're all wondering a little. Diego has never brought any girl over before. Not even for dinner. And suddenly he's moving one in?" Tammy left the question hanging, then continued, "It's more than a little disconcerting. Maybe for Casey more than Tom and me. Tom thinks that she may have deeper feelings for him." Tammy tilted her head and her gaze seemed to bore straight into Amy. "We all just want to make sure you're in this relationship for the right reasons."

"I am," Amy said simply. She'd read somewhere that if you were going to lie then do it in a few words as possible.

"Good." The smile returned to Tammy's face but didn't spread to her eyes. "Let's get you back upstairs. I'm sure you want to settle in. Diego will be home soon and finally in a good mood since the Atoms won."

"I know. He scored the go-ahead goal. The drought's over."

"From your lips, sweetie. From your lips."

As Amy unpacked, her worries came back to haunt her. How could someone live for twenty-five years on God's green earth and have so little to show for it? Was she that much of a failure? She'd packed her clothes, toiletries, a few books, and her mother's pearls. Everything else her parents had left was in storage. The second she shut the door on the storage unit she'd closed off her own life. Looking at the half-empty suitcase before her, she realized there wasn't much to her.

She felt hollow. Tammy's warnings had unnerved her. The woman was blunt, if nothing else. In Knight's living room, the proposition had seemed like a way out of her current drudgery. Now she was achingly aware that real people with real feelings could be hurt by this, and Simon had been her wakeup call.

And finally, there was Casey. Not having enough information had nearly blown her cover. That was Paul Knight's fault. But fixating on how nice the PA's ass looked in sopping wet jeans was a problem all of her own making. She was in trouble. She could already feel the anxious flutter in her chest.

A sharp knock at the door disturbed her thoughts.

"Who is it?" Amy asked.

"Casey. Sorry to bother you."

Amy froze then quickly fluffed up her hair and pinched her sallow cheeks in the mirror. She hesitated. What was wrong with her? She was having the fake relationship with Diego, not Casey.

When she answered the door, she couldn't even look Casey in the eyes. Her gaze fell away to the lean, hard body. Casey had changed into an Atoms T-shirt, shorts, and black and purple flip flops. A delicate soccer ball tattoo rode her left ankle. Amy's eyes lingered on the design for a long moment. Sexy.

"Here."

Amy looked up to catch the single sheet of white paper Casey thrust out to her.

"Knight wanted me to give you Diego's schedule for tomorrow. There's a photo shoot for Adidas in the morning, and a televised publicity event at the park in the afternoon. There will be press cameras at the park, if that makes a difference to you."

"Should it?" She met a cold, hard stare. A jolt ran through her body. What had happened by the pool was happening again up here. It was inexplicable. Her body was reacting in a way that her mind couldn't stop.

"I thought you might want to dress for the photo op. Diego will be in his Adidas stuff, of course, but you can come however you want." Casey's eyes narrowed slightly, making Amy feel like an ant at a picnic.

"Okay. Thanks." They stood awkwardly in the doorway and regarded each other in silence.

"Look, if you give me your information, I can just text you the schedule next time," Casey said. "That way I won't have to bother you in person."

"Sure. That works for me." *I'm a liar on all fronts now.* That zap of lust, guilt, confusion, whatever it was, left her tingling all over. It was vaguely uncomfortable. It was also the first time she had felt something really physical for over two years.

Casey swiped open her cell phone and handed it to Amy who quickly entered her contact information.

"Hey, you two." Diego in all his casual glory strode along the hall. Dulce trotted along at his heels. His smile shifted ever so slightly as he met them in the doorway.

Amy's brow furrowed. Their first meeting in their new home was about to be witnessed by his PA. They were unrehearsed, and unless they got really lucky, a lot could go wrong. Amy struggled for the right words. "You scored. I saw the goal. It was great!"

Diego's shoulders visibly relaxed. Soccer was the perfect subject. They could both be enthusiastic about it, and maybe fool Casey into thinking that they were being enthusiastic about each other.

"It was a garbage goal. I was lucky to be in the right place at the right time. But I'll take anything right now. It's so good to see you, here." He swept past Casey to take Amy in his arms. He gave her a delicate hug picking her up and cradling her for a moment. He dipped his head down to hers to whisper softly in a voice only she could hear. "I'm going to kiss you now."

He dropped her back to her toes and planted a kiss that was more noise than touch on her lips.

Amy grinned. Who knew Diego would be so good at this? A lifetime of hiding his sexual identity would make anyone an expert actor, she guessed.

"It was a good goal, Diego. It's all about positioning," Casey said, as soon as they broke from each other.

Amy noticed that her face softened as she looked at him. What was it Tammy had said? Something about liking him too much?

He slung an arm around Casey and gave her a quick side hug. "I don't care what kind of goal it was as long as it gets the reporters off my back. That's all I really need right now." He swept them into the apartment. Dulce nipped playfully at Amy's feet as they moved. "You settling in all right? Have everything you need?"

"I do. It's wonderful. And so is this little one." She bent down to pick up the wriggling dog.

"She's a very good judge of character. So I'm happy to see she adores you. Just like me." Diego stroked Dulce as she snuggled into Amy's arms.

"I'll let you two have some privacy," Casey said in a voice a little too loud. She moved back to the hallway, shutting the door behind her.

Diego jumped back a step as he put a finger up to his lips. He silently mouthed counting to ten and then broke out into a shy smile. "That was good!"

"Oh my God." Amy giggled. "I didn't know what to do."

"I know. I thought it might be over before we started. Casey's pretty shrewd. Talking about the goal was a stroke of brilliance."

"You picked up the lead. I think this fake relationship might really go the distance."

He grinned at her. "Well, right now the only distance I want to travel is to the backyard. Tammy's set out dinner for us. You ready to eat?"

"Sure, that sounds great." Their first dinner together. Amy's heart raced as if it were a real date. Obviously nothing romantic would come of it, but the evening would set the tone for their entire relationship. It was off to a great start. Now she had to make sure it stayed there. She eased Dulce from her arms and followed Diego downstairs.

A romantic dinner for two graced one of the patios. Two plates of grilled chicken breast with sides of zucchini and carrots sat on a small bistro-style table, complete with lit candles. Spray mist cooled the air, taking the heat in the patio area down from unbearable to balmy.

"It's not just sugar I avoid, I try to eat healthy at all times," Diego said, almost apologizing for the food. Tammy came out with sparkling water in a wine cooler which she placed on the table. "As you know, of course," he added.

"I do. Remember when the server didn't believe that you had ordered the salad and not me?" She turned her attention to Tammy. "I had to reach for the hamburger off his plate, before the server realized we weren't joking. It looks great, Tammy."

"I know what he likes to eat. He's my boy."

"Good cover," Diego said softly, as Tammy returned to the kitchen.

"I think it'll get it easier to keep up the charade as we go along," Amy said, as she watched Tammy take up sentry at the kitchen window to keep an eye on them. Then she dropped her gaze to the beautifully plated meal. Far better than the prawn-flavored chips she and Simon used to steal from Reggie's for dinner.

"I hope so. I need to start playing better. Get my stats up. This has been a really difficult spell for me."

"You could change that. You could come out. It might help." She said the words before she realized how very stupid they were. "Sorry!" Her face went red. It wasn't as if that solution was even revolutionary. Obviously, he would have considered and dismissed that scenario long before Knight found him a beard. "I'm talking myself out of a good gig." She tried to lighten her gaff.

"It's okay. If this is going to work, at least you and I have to be honest with each other."

She studied Diego. He was right. They had to keep their relationship as authentic and as candid as this bizarre situation would allow. But did he mean it? They had grown closer since their first meeting at Knight's house. Even though little alarm bells rang in her head, she decided to take a chance. "Okay, so why don't you?"

"I just can't," Diego said, sighing. He seemed relieved to talk about it, but still he spun the dial on his expensive diver's watch as his gaze drifted away from her eyes. "I mean I've thought about it, of course. There's times that I would like nothing better. But I take care of my entire family. Financially, I mean, through all these damn endorsement deals. It's about so much more than me."

"But professional athletes are coming out these days." She pushed the conversation right to the edge. Why couldn't she just shut up? Everything had been going so well, and now she might get fired before the meal was over. She put a piece of chicken smothered in creamy mustard sauce into her mouth so she couldn't speak anymore.

"Some are. Mostly after their careers are over. Very few are coming out before they're superstars. That college basketball player, for example. He came out right after he graduated and dropped at least three rounds in the draft because of it, or so some people said."

"True."

"Besides, if I was white, it might be different. But I'm the face of Hispanic advertising. Latinos and Latinas want to connect with brands that embrace their culture. For better and for worse, I'm that brand. And there's the problem. I need to connect to both the traditionalists and the second generation-plus. At least that's what they tell me."

"Sorry?"

"It's two completely different demographics. Traditionalists are immigrants who arrive here with all of their ideas shaped by the culture of Mexico. The rest of us are second, third, and fourth generations. We're more American in our likes and dislikes." His tone was sure, but he spun the dial on his watch like a top. "You see. I'm hip, I speak English as well as any native." He grinned ruefully.

"Better." Amy finally found a word that didn't flirt with trouble.

"Thanks. So far my endorsement deals are only with the brands that do well with Hispanics. I need a Nike, or Gatorade, or Levi to be really safe."

"And your fans? They wouldn't support you?"

"Are you kidding me? For Christ's sake, Mexican fans chant puto, or faggot, at games when a player makes a bad move. And FIFA's not doing anything about it. They say it's not discriminatory in this particular context."

His words hung in the air between them. It sounded to Amy that, despite what Knight thought, Diego had a handle on more than looking like a movie star and producing on the field. "So you're stuck in this and all sorts of other lies?"

"That's about the size of it. It would be nice if all this were about playing soccer, which I love. But I haven't had that feeling about soccer since high school."

The swooshing as the patio door opened brought the conversation to an end. Tammy produced the dessert, sweet summer strawberries with whipped cream.

"Ah, my favorite," Diego said, grabbing a bright red strawberry.

"Well, I knew you weren't going to eat much with the photo shoot tomorrow." Tammy picked up his half-eaten plate of food. "Shirt off, I gather?"

"No, but it's skin-tight. And I wasn't being vain." He laughed. "I was talking too much." He threw a shy glance at Amy.

They waited while Tammy cleared the plates and left. Then when she reappeared at the kitchen window, Diego put his hand on Amy's. From inside they would look like any couple courting. Strategy had always been Diego's strong suit, on and off the field.

"This evening went better than I hoped. I like the fact that there's someone in my life that I don't have to pretend with." He considered her for a moment. "You don't have to come tomorrow, but I think I would like to have you there anyway. Is that weird?"

"Then I'll be there."

Diego grinned his thousand-watt smile.

Amy realized she was invested in this job more than she thought she could be. The big bonus being that if she played her cards right she might never have to say, "Next guest in line, please," ever again.

It was the picture-perfect ending to the fake date. She hadn't gotten fired, the conversation was interesting, the chicken tasted far better than prawn potato chips, and Diego and she might actually be on the way to becoming friends. What was she worried about? She could totally do this.

CHAPTER 4

THE TENSION STARTED ALMOST IMMEDIATELY the next morning. Adidas sent a town car to take them to the photo shoot. Diego, Casey, and Amy piled into the backseat. Casey slid in first; then Diego helped Amy inside, but it became clear the three of them couldn't all fit comfortably. They were crammed in like sardines, and Amy's left leg, from hip to knee, rode Casey's thigh next to her. It felt firm and warm under the thin material of her linen pants, and Amy tried to shut out that awareness. But she made no move to ease the pressure.

"I'll get in front," Casey said quickly, and slid out her door, taking a place with the driver up front. She let her back fall heavily against the seat and crossed her arms over her chest. "This is better. Shall we go?"

Amy took it all in. She would have to be careful about Casey. She had literally just taken her spot in the backseat and pushed her up with the "help." Who could feel good about that? But that wasn't the only thing she'd have to be careful of. Amy slid her hand down the empty space where

Casey's leg had been seconds before. She could still feel the heat where their bodies had touched.

Luckily, Diego gave an interview on his cellphone for the rest of the drive, and nobody had to make small talk. Amy couldn't hear the questions the reporter posed, but Diego's answers were perfect.

"Sometimes you go through a spell where you don't score. Soccer's just like that. Every sport is, I guess." He sounded calm, but his foot tapped restlessly on the floor of the car. "No, I don't credit Amy. I mean, she's great and all that." He smiled at her. "But I'm the same player that I was before I met her. That's just how the game is. You can't chase it. If you're not doing well individually, then you got to find other ways to contribute. In the end, it's about the team, not the individual."

Amy stopped listening when she realized that she'd been staring at the back of Casey's neck the whole time. Now she really took it in. Slender, strong, touchable.

She turned away and looked pensively out the window. As Diego had said, it was all about the team, and she was part of team Diego now. That meant there was no place for all these dangerous feelings that were starting to bubble up inside her.

The tension continued to escalate as soon as they walked into the studio. The Adidas advertising executives, Paul Knight, and Lucy

Lewitt, Diego's publicist, descended like vultures. Each one reached out to pull Diego into a corner for a private conversation. When they couldn't all grab him at once, they turned their talons on Casey. "Could you please," started every demand. The words shot at Casey as if they were pecking at her. In response, she flew around the studio ordering coffee, changing schedules, calling people to the set—all menial tasks they could have easily performed themselves. It was a pissing contest to see who had the most power in their little group, and Casey was their battlefield.

Diego was oblivious to it all. He threw Amy an air kiss as someone from Adidas took him into a dressing room to change for the shoot.

Amy caught the air kiss in her outstretched fist and brought it up to her lips. Out of the corner of her eye, she saw Knight nodding ever so slightly to himself. Then she noticed a pretty young intern give Diego a hungry look and her a spiteful one. All good.

Lucy Lewitt sidled up to Amy and put a dainty hand on her shoulder. "You're good for him." Lucy's voice was surprisingly childlike.

"And he's good for me."

Lucy smiled and continued, "We should get some shots of you two today for the Twitter feed. Do you mind?"

"Not at all."

"Great. Casey?"

On the other side of the set, Casey turned to her with a withering look that was lost on Lucy.

"Could you please get the Adidas people to get Amy some gear? One of those aerodynamic tops that Diego is changing into, I think." She dismissed Casey with a wave of her hand.

"I can do that," Amy said quickly. Her developing feelings for Casey aside, she didn't like the way that Lucy was treating her. It reeked too much of the Reggie treatment, which she hoped she had left behind her in the Valley Arms.

"Don't be silly, dear. That's her job."

"I'm pretty sure it isn't."

"Of course it is." Lucy laughed as if Amy were crazy.

Amy scanned the room. She had no idea who to approach for the clothes and so in the end had to go to Casey, herself. She touched her lightly on her arm.

"Sorry, but who do I ask?"

Casey sighed. "I don't need you fighting my battles for me." Her tone could cut glass.

"I didn't do it for you. I did it for me. I've been there." Finally, she said something that wasn't a lie. "Just because you work for someone, or in this case don't work for them, doesn't make them better than you." Amy looked into Casey's eyes. No thawing.

Casey did check out the room, however. "Francine? Sorry to bother you. Do we have any of those Adidas tops that Diego is wearing that would fit her?" She pointed at Amy.

Her? How hard would it have been to use my name? Same amount of letters and all.

A heavyset woman tugged at the measuring tape around her neck and pursed her lips. "Hmm, let me call over to wardrobe?"

"Thank you, Francine." Casey inclined her head to the woman, who smiled back at her.

"Thanks, Casey," Amy added, noting that the Adidas team seemed to really like her.

When Diego came back from the make-up chair, all heads, including Amy's, turned in his direction.

"Ta-da!" He threw his arms up high over his head in his excitement. The skin-tight Adidas workout shirt and compression shorts hugged his body and showed off the long, lean muscles of an incredibly fit soccer player. Francine waddled over to Diego to tie off the shirt in the back to make it even tighter. Washboard abs leaped to life under the material, and the young intern giggled with appreciation.

"Too tight? Can you move?" Francine asked and ran her hand all the way around Diego's waist.

"Barely. But I'm good."

Francine touched him a few more times, and Amy got the feeling that she was enjoying her job almost too much. Amy didn't blame her. The outfit left nothing to the imagination, and frankly, no one's imagination could do any better. He was the cover boy of ancient Greek aesthetics with his Adonis body.

"Okay! Let's do this thing!" he said.

A palpable energy pulsed through the room. Everyone smiled at Diego and then at each other. Amy remembered her college soccer coach's favorite quote. "A really good player doesn't even have to touch the ball to affect the game. She just needs to make everyone else believe that when the ball comes to them, they can put it in the back of the net." Diego had done just that.

A tall, thin man with glasses slapped Diego on the back and took him to the green screen that dominated the back third of the room.

"That's Ryan, the creative director. A good director always makes the talent feel comfortable, but Ryan takes it to a whole new level," a soft voice said directly behind Amy. She didn't need to turn around to know it was Knight. That creepy feeling she had for him had reached her even before his words. "I think he has a little something for our boy. Can you take care of it?"

"I'll try." That's what he was paying her for after all, but taking care of it didn't sit well with Amy as she moved toward Diego. If Ryan did like Diego, a fake girlfriend wasn't going fool him. Queers knew their own. Ryan kept his hand on Diego's shoulder as he ran though the poses on the shot list. As the hand began to slide down Diego's back, Amy saw Knight flinch, so she sidled in between them and Ryan was forced off to the side.

"This whole set-up is amazing," Amy said.

Diego met her gaze as embarrassment flashed in his eyes. Amy realized that he liked Ryan's attention, but understood he shouldn't allow himself to. Her heart went out to him, and she touched his arm.

"Diego, we're ready for you. Could you take your place, please?" Ryan said curtly, breaking up the moment.

Diego stood in front of the screen with his arm stretched out, palm up. Ryan positioned the new hi-tech Adidas ball, which registered the speed and trajectory of a strike, on the palm of his hand.

"Pull up the star field," Ryan said to a man hovering over a computer.

A million twinkling stars popped into existence behind Diego on the screen. With a simple click of a mouse, Diego was a superman hovering in space offering the ball to the consumer. Diego's jaw was set, but the glint in his eye seemed to say, "Buy the ball, train hard, and you, too, can play like me."

"Excellent," Ryan said. Amy stood looking over his shoulder.

"He's a natural," she said.

Ryan studied her for a moment. "Yes, he's perfect," he said, finally. Amy caught the double meaning. He was telling her that he knew about Diego's true nature.

"I know." She raised her eyebrows and smiled to give her statement an enigmatic twist. Then she walked away to make sure she had the last word. *Knight's crazy if he thinks this is going to work.*

Soon, though, the excitement of the shoot overtook her concerns. Camera's clicked; Ryan shouted directions. Diego laughed and chatted his way through the morning. No wonder everyone wanted a piece of him. People just felt better when he was around.

At one point, Francine reappeared, thrust several items of clothing into Amy's arms and pointed to the small dressing room. Amy held up a tiny shirt.

"Um. I'm not sure this is my size."

"It's close enough," Francine said. "They're made to show off the body. Go try it on. You might like what you see. I know Diego will."

Amy did as she was told. She wriggled into the shorts and then squeezed the shirt down over her chest inch by inch. It was ridiculously tight, exposing every flaw. Amy had believed that she was more or less in shape from all her jogging and bike riding. The shirt cupped her breasts and stomach like a glove. Sadly, it also exposed how soft she had become in the two years since she'd left the soccer field and instituted Margarita Mondays at the bar. She considered her reflection in the mirror. *I would rather go out there naked than in these clothes.*

There was a soft tap on the dressing room door. "They're ready for you." Casey's voice drifted in, void of all emotion.

"Sorry, but can you tell Francine that I need another shirt? I'm not coming out like this."

Casey yanked open the door without warning. Her gaze traveled up and down Amy's body as if she were a sculptor looking at a lump of untapped marble. "You look fine."

Amy, in a knee jerk reaction, rapidly pushed the door shut in her face. "Casey, can you please tell Francine to get me a looser shirt." In her embarrassment, she ordered Casey around like everyone else.

A quick look in the mirror told her what she already knew. Her face and arms were a deep red. She hadn't meant to be that curt with Casey, but she also hadn't intended for anyone to see her like this.

Casey had heard her loud and clear. A hand clutching a bright green Adidas training tee slipped around the dressing room door a few minutes later.

"Thanks," Amy mumbled.

Casey said nothing.

"Time is money, sweetie." Lucy came knocking on the door moments later. The T-shirt was a much better look for her. The bright color made her complexion glow, and it was just loose enough to hide her flaws without creating a tent effect. Lucy took her by the elbow and guided her to the hair and make-up station a few feet away.

"There you go," she said, directing Amy into the chair. "Pull her hair back and stay natural, I think. Maybe even out her tone and define her eyes a little bit more," she told the stylist.

Amy usually got ready in the morning in under ten minutes and was surprised how much she enjoyed being pampered. Her hair was restyled as a messy ponytail that looked like she had pulled her hair into a scrunchie that morning without a thought. The make-up girl designed a natural look that Amy soon realized was anything but artless. She checked her reflection in the mirror. Success! She looked like she put the F in fun.

When she finally made it to the green screen, Diego gave a low whistle. "You look great."

"Who knew," she said casually, but secretly she glowed with her transformation. She looked around to see if Casey had noticed, but she was talking to another woman with her back to her.

"Okay." Lucy marched center stage to take control. "So you play soccer too, Amy?"

"I do."

"Can you do that...what's it called? That thing where you bounce the ball on your foot and your leg?"

"You mean juggling?"

"Yes, that."

"I can."

Lucy clapped her hands in delight. "So clear back everyone and let them juggle." No one moved. The crew looked to Ryan, who looked to Knight, who nodded. Amy wouldn't have guessed that Knight out of all these people was the top of the power pyramid, but a simple nod from him got everyone moving. Before she knew it, she and Diego were bobbing the ball back and forth to each other in front of the extended green screen. Diego, at first, had given her simple transfers with no spin right to her feet.

"You're going easy on me," she said. She flipped the ball behind her back to heel kick it over to Diego.

Diego's eyes widened, and some of the studio guys whistled and clapped.

"Game on!" Diego cried, and matched her trick with one of his own. The ball flew between them like lightning, and very soon she was outclassed. The camera clicked at a steady rate until Ryan called from the back of the room. "That's a wrap, guys. We got what we need."

So had Amy. When she tapped the ball to the production assistant, she looked up to see the first crack in Casey's persona. The chill was still in her eyes, but her expression was thoughtful. Amy met her gaze, trying to get beyond her defenses. She would have given all the money she now had in the bank to know what that look meant.

Diego fell back on the couch. They were back home hanging out in the den after a full day. Tammy and Tom had retired for the evening so they had the house to themselves. The atmosphere seemed lighter with the Winters' absence. Soft music played in the background, and Dulce lay cuddled between them.

"Thank you. I've never had so much fun on a PR day," Diego said, idly stroking the dog's silky ears.

"I've never had a PR day," Amy said. She was slumped beside him. "They're exhausting."

"Well, trust me they're usually a lot more tedious. Thank you for playing with me and the kids at the park. You were really good."

"It was my pleasure. I'd forgotten how much fun a kick-around is."

Amy ran the events of the afternoon through her mind. Diego had returned to his childhood soccer field, no more than a dirt-and-weed pitch at a local park sandwiched between run-down apartment buildings. Knight and Lucy Lewitt had carefully handpicked the local kids for the shoot months ago. It all looked so coincidental. Diego sauntered up and stopped an out of bounds ball, then asked, "Hey, guys, can I play?"

The kids screamed and piled onto Diego for a group hug. The TV cameras ate up everything. When Knight was sure the cameras were pointed at Amy he gave her a little shove.

"Go play with them."

"I don't have any shoes." She looked down to her slip-on flats.

"Casey? Could you please get Amy some shoes?" He gave the inevitable command.

Soft, expensive turf shoes appeared like magic, and just as if she were Cinderella, fit perfectly. Amy trotted onto the field as if she had worn them all her life.

"Girls against boys!" she called. The girls ran to her side of the makeshift pitch, and the game was on.

The ball was at her feet, she slid it between the legs of one of the older boys who had thought himself above playing against girls.

"Oye, chamaco! Mira la pelota, no a la chica! They're too good." Diego nudged the boy out of his embarrassment, before he took off down the field.

"That's right!" The lanky girl goalie at the back of the field called out. Amy caught her eye and they shared a nod.

Amy was sure that Diego had somehow engineered the girls' victory. But it was good for everyone on the field and even better for the cameras on the sideline.

"You know I thought it was kinda silly." Amy settled back into the couch in the den. "Who would actually buy that you would just show up at a field with more rocks than grass and play with a bunch of kids on your day off? The whole thing was nothing more than a ridiculous stunt for TV."

Diego's smile froze and a guarded look crept across his face. Amy could've kicked herself.

"No, no," she said. "I mean I thought it was silly as a promo stunt. But then I saw the kids actually got something out of it. That goalie on my team was more than good. I talked to her after. You know, she's only in middle school. So I told her to try out for the high school team next year. And who knows, if she continues to improve, there's college scholarships and club teams and even Olympic development programs. You know, a good goalie can pretty much write her own ticket and she..."

She looked up to see the guarded look long gone. Diego's smile was back and in full force. Amy clamped her mouth shut so hard her teeth snapped into each other. What was she thinking? Rambling on and on. Lecturing Diego Torres on soccer.

Diego only laughed. "That's why I agree to those," and he air quoted, "ridiculous promo stunts." He stretched his long legs out across the coffee table and got comfortable. "It's not for the TV or for spiking my publicity. When I was a kid, much younger than those kids were, my brothers and I were messing around with a ball at that same park. There was this guy who was running laps around the field. He was training as it turned out, but he stopped and watched us for a while. I guess I was doing something that caught his attention, because he told me that I was really good. He played for the local college team, and he told me to keep practicing, because they could really use good players."

"And that made a difference?"

"All the difference. This guy, who probably forgot about me as soon as he got home, planted a seed. College. No one in my family had ever gone to college. We lived in a tiny apartment above the self-storage facility my dad managed. Soccer was just a way for my mom to get me and my brothers out of her hair. But I started really practicing from that moment on." He shrugged. "You never know what makes a difference to a kid."

"You were really good with them," he continued. "And I'm not just talking about your moves, although you do have a wicked first touch. They liked you. We should get Paul on it. Create more opportunities for you to do some real good in all these bogus situations."

"I'd really like that." A little laugh escaped her lips. Helping kids would certainly make her feel she'd earned her paycheck. "How about an after school homework and soccer club? There's lots of ways to get to college, and I've always wanted to work with kids in some way."

"We'll text Paul tomorrow."

"That'd be great." She patted his arm. She was touched he would do this for her.

She imagined the facility they might create. A colorful room full of posters and supplies. She could tutor in English and history and help out with writing in any subject. On breaks they could go out and kick a ball around on a grassy field right outside the door. It was a simple idea, but with Diego's name and money behind it, who knew what could come out of it.

They both noticed almost simultaneously her hand still resting on his arm. Her fingers curled idly around his forearm. She yanked her hand away. Shit. She didn't want Diego to think she had designs on him. Nothing could be further from the truth.

"Sorry," she said, and her cheeks flushed.

"Nothing to apologize for." But Diego slid his feet off the coffee table and stood up. He went over to the large fireplace and casually examined the photographs grouped on the mantelpiece. Suddenly, the whole thing felt a lot like a real relationship. Amy had overstepped, and Diego was now pushing back to regain the space between them.

"Well, I got a big day tomorrow." Diego idly fingered a picture of him kissing an older Latina woman on the cheek. "It's a fitness day. I'm hitting the gym early with my trainer and then down to the stadium. The guys and I will probably go out to eat afterwards. I take the rookies out once a week. You know their salaries are shit." Diego slid the picture back and forth across the mantelpiece. "Just the guys usually. You could join us, I guess, if you wanted?"

Amy studied him for a moment. Was this a command appearance? Was the boss setting up a meeting or was he just being nice? Diego continued to fidget.

"Oh, thanks. But I'm good." She took a shot in the dark.

Diego smiled and moved toward the hallway. Amy relaxed; she'd made the right move.

"You'll be okay, all by yourself for the whole day?" he asked.

"I will." She smiled to let him know she was really fine with it.

"Good. Hang out by the pool. Relax while you can. I have Friday off, and we've a command performance at my parents' house. They all want to meet my fiancée, you know." He said it lightly, as if meeting his entire family were no big deal.

Amy's heart started to pound. "Really?"

"Don't worry. My mother says she understands why I kept you a secret. It'll be fun."

"Okay." Amy wasn't convinced. She'd known this was coming, but she sure wasn't ready for it. Diego had more on the line here. How could he be so okay with it? Should she call him on it? For starting out so well, the day was disintegrating fast.

"Can I walk you to your room?" Diego brought the evening to a close.

"No. I'm good."

"Great. Goodnight, then." He blew her a kiss goodnight, his go-to move at intimacy between them, and called Dulce to him. The mutt looked back and forth between Amy and Diego and sat down on her haunches.

Diego laughed as he left. "Traitor," he softly scolded the little dog.

Amy sat on in the den. The room seemed so much bigger now Diego had gone; his presence was like that. She looked at the various photos on the mantelpiece. Most were of his family, in some he stood with his teammates, and there was one of him standing on white sand in front of a beautiful ocean. He looked larger than life.

Dulce whined, and Amy picked her up. The little dog was her only ally in this new game. She buried her face in the soft fur. Dulce smelled of dog shampoo and something else, something wonderfully earthy and natural. The dog snuggled into her arms with a contented groan.

"Come on, let's go upstairs, sweet one."

In the kitchenette her phone beeped. She shoved her cocoa mug into the microwave and reached for it. For a second, she hoped Simon had finally answered her texts.

"OMG. I just saw a promo of U and D on TV. UR FAMOUS! Let's get together!"

Not Simon, then. It was Blythe, the assistant store manager at her Starbucks. Blythe hadn't given her the time of day when she worked there, and now a text? Knight had warned her about this kind of thing.

"People will come out of the woodwork when they see you with Diego," he had told her. "They'll all want a piece of you. Stay away from them."

Amy deleted the text and dropped the phone back on the counter. She didn't like a world where Paul Knight knew how it all fit together better than she did.

"Come on, Dulce. Let's go to bed."

CHAPTER 5

"You're done studying," Darla said softly.

"I have a paper due," Amy protested, but she knew it was futile.

"Well I have something else due. Or someone else to do, should I say."

Amy's chest fizzed with excitement. Darla moved to her side. She dropped her hand on Amy's shoulder and slid it down her bare arm until their fingers entwined. A soft tug. The book slid from her grasp. Another soft tug. She was up and out of her chair.

"Come on."

"Where we going?"

"Places you've only dreamed of." Darla smiled. Her grip on Amy's hand tightened. Then they were moving through the library. Tall stacks towering above them and the passageway growing narrower and darker.

Darla's amber eyes sparked with desire. She cupped Amy's cheek then delicately traced a fingertip along her jaw and pushed a strand of hair away from her neck. The gesture was so simple but so intimate. Slowly, she pushed her back against the wall.

"You smell like books and grass and sun."

"That's all I do." Amy's response was little more than a breath.

Darla kissed her neck. "But I taste something else. Do you know what it is?" She dropped to her knees. Her hands drifted along the back of Amy's thighs, up under her dress.

Amy was shaking. Her legs trembled so much they could barely support her.

"Can you tell me?" Her voice was soft and seductive. Her hands moved like silk over Amy's behind and rested there.

"No." Amy dropped her gaze to Darla's face. It transfixed her. Her skin glowed like polished mahogany in the dim light.

Darla slid her hands inside Amy's panties. The heat from Darla's palms was intense on the cool skin of her backside.

"Should I show you?"

"Please," Amy whispered. She tipped her head back against the concrete wall and let its coolness seep into her back. She was burning up. Heat pulsed in waves through her body. Darla's fingers grazed her damp sex. Amy shuddered with pleasure.

"I taste desire." Darla spread her legs wider. "And you." Slowly, excruciatingly she moved toward her center.

"Please." Amy breathed.

Darla moaned in response and slid a finger deep into Amy. She shuddered, ripples of sensation coursed through her. She tightened around Darla's strokes, the friction building a delicious tension throughout her body. All that existed was this space between her legs and the exquisite touch of her first lover. The girl who had taught her who she really was. Darla stroked slowly, sensually, in and out, adding another finger when she sensed Amy was ready.

"Look at me."

Amy slid down the wall, sinking onto Darla's hand, moving into her rhythm, wanting more, building, building—

"Look at me."

Amy opened her eyes and stared at Darla. Her amber eyes were light and sparkling, not dark at all. And then they turned blue. They burned through her with longing, and the blue was like a horizon that seemed to go on forever.

"Casey?" Amy struggled to speak.

"We both know I'm the one you really want." Casey was holding her against the wall. Casey was pushing into her body, priming it, making her explode. Casey was—

Metal slammed against metal.

Amy's eyes flew open.

The stacks. Casey. Her building orgasm. All gone. Slipping away from her and back into the land of dreams.

What the hell was that noise?

Now that her mind was clearing, it only took a second to realize that it came from Diego's home gym. The weight machines were right under her apartment. She took a deep breath, trying to orient herself. Dulce began yipping to be let out. Amy pulled herself out of bed and opened the door a crack. The dog shot out like a bullet. The clanking echoed louder in the hallway. *Shit, for the amount of money this place cost can't Diego afford better soundproofing?*

She headed for the bathroom, hoping a hot shower would improve her mood. In the shower stall, she inadvertently leaned against one of the buttons and steam tinged with the fresh scent of eucalyptus enveloped her. Another one of the luxurious treats living at casa Diego brought. Any other day, Amy would have adored the aromatherapy treatment but this morning being transported to an eucalyptus forest took her further away from Casey and her sexy dream. She dropped her hand between her thighs, hoping to recapture the magic. Nope. The sparkle had definitely gone. With a sigh she reached for the shampoo.

Dressed and ready for the day Amy headed downstairs. She took a quick look in the gym to see Diego pumping weights at a chest press machine. A very handsome man with slick blond hair stood over him counting down the reps. "You can do it, man. Come on!"

Amy pulled back quickly before either of them turned to see her at the door. She had the distinct feeling that she was watching a private moment. Not really knowing where to go, she aimlessly wandered into the kitchen. The smell of freshly brewed coffee hit her as soon as she walked in. Tammy sat at the oversized table, reading the newspaper and drinking from a steaming cup.

"Morning, Tammy."

"Morning," she answered, without looking up.

"Is there any more coffee."

"In the pot. And there's eggs and toast as well."

"You really didn't have to make me breakfast."

"Oh, I didn't, sweetie." She made sweetie sound cold. "I fixed it for Diego, but there's some leftover."

"Well then, how can I say no?"

"It's in the steamer."

Amy glanced around the kitchen looking for something that could be a steamer. She opened the dishwasher, a refrigeration drawer filled with energy drinks, and finally the warming drawer. Nestled inside was a perfectly portioned breakfast of fluffy eggs and buttered toast. She reached out to grab the plate, and then jerked her hand back. It was scorching hot.

"Careful, the plate's hot," Tammy said from behind her paper.

Amy had the distinct feeling that Tammy was grinning ear to ear. She grabbed a dish towel and brought the plate to the table, sitting down on the other side, staking out her own territory.

Tammy folded her paper. "So what are you going to do today?"

"I don't know. Diego will be at the stadium. I gather that's for the whole day." Time stretched out in front of her. What was she going to do all day? She was pretty sure that Tammy wasn't going to sit around and throw ice cubes with her the way Simon had. "Maybe I'll—"

"Today is a big cleaning day for me. You'll need to stay out of my way."

"Okay," she said, not letting Tammy push her buttons. "You got any suggestions about what I could do?"

"*I* do. I've been thinking about it." Diego sauntered into the kitchen with a towel hung around his neck. He was flushed and glowed with sweat and good health. His trainer followed close on his heels but stopped short when he saw Amy.

Tammy slapped down the paper and jumped to her feet. "Antioxidant smoothie?" she offered.

"Yes, please," Diego said, turning to face Amy. "I have an idea for you. I'm sending Casey out to this crazy place in Oxnard. It's a golf course where you kick a soccer ball instead of hitting a golf ball. Do you want to go?"

Tammy turned on the blender so Amy had to almost shout her response. "Really? That's a thing?" The trainer moved closer to Diego, and

Amy wondered for split second what it was like for Diego to have Tammy and this handsome man orbit him as if he were the sun.

"Oh," Diego said, suddenly remembering the introductions. "Rob, this is Amy, my fiancée. Amy, this is Rob, my trainer."

"Good to meet you, Rob," Amy said.

Rob raised a hand in a halfhearted greeting. "Hi, Amy." But he had already dismissed her even as he said her name. He swung back toward Diego. "I gotta get going, man."

"Cool. See you Thursday." Diego took a glass of something very green out of Tammy's outstretched hand.

Rob let himself out, and Amy watched as Diego's gaze followed him all the way down the path and around the corner. Diego was zeroing in on his ass. Amy bit her lip and frowned. Diego couldn't afford slip-ups like this if their deception was going to work.

Tammy was staring at her from across the kitchen. Their gazes locked before Tammy quickly looked away.

Amy's stomach lurched. What had Tammy seen?

"I'm going to take a shower, then head down to the stadium." Diego downed the last of his smoothie. He smiled at both women, oblivious to the atmosphere in the room. "I'll call you later, babe," he called over his shoulder to Amy.

"Can't wait."

Amy sagged back in her seat, grateful that Diego had forgotten about Oxnard. She silently thanked Rob for having such a cute ass. So cute that Diego's plans for her and Casey had slipped his mind.

Diego popped his head back around the doorpost almost on cue. "I know it sounds ridiculous, Amy, but that course wants my endorsement. They're part of an actual league. Will you check it out with Casey? Paul thinks Nike may even sign on as sponsor and this may be our way in with them."

A full day with Casey. Not a good idea. "I don't want to cramp her style." Even to her ears she sounded lame.

"You won't. I'm sure she'd really like the company. And it will be a hell of lot cooler up by the beach. Actually, I'd really like for you to go and give me your true opinion. Play a round and tell me what you think. Is this something I should get involved in?"

Now the outing was an official request. No wiggle room. "Sure. I'd love to. I'm always up for something new." Amy hoped she had hit the right, light note.

"That's my girl," Diego said, and came back in to give her a quick kiss on the lips. "Sorry, I'm a little sweaty. Here. Don't move." He playfully patted her mouth with the towel. Tammy and Amy watched him head off for his shower.

"I guess I'm going to Oxnard." Amy fixed Tammy with a cool stare to see if she could read anything in the older woman's face.

"I think Casey's already out in the office. You better go tell her." Tammy looked disinterested.

Amy rose to take her empty plate to the sink.

"I'll get that," Tammy said. "You better skedaddle. You wouldn't want her to leave without you."

"Okay. Thanks for breakfast."

"Whenever Diego's in town, I'll put a plate in the warmer for when you don't get to eat together."

"Don't go to any trouble."

"I'm cooking anyways. It's no trouble."

Amy suspected Tammy had hit on an ingenious way to keep tabs on when she and Diego ate together, like any newly engaged couple would. And, more importantly, when they didn't. It was the thin end of a wedge that could throw up other discrepancies in their routines.

The nagging feeling that Tammy might be a snake followed her out of the house and across the flagstone patio towards the office. Through the glass doors Amy could see Casey on her knees before a bookshelf. Her fingers tapped across the three-ring binders until she found the one she wanted. Everything fell out of focus. Casey on her knees. The shelf of books. The resonance of her dream echoed through her as if it had been some kind of premonition.

Then the glass doors slid open and Casey said, "Yes?"

Her voice seemed to come from far away, and was distorted, as if she were under water. This is ridiculous. Amy struggled to get a hold of herself. This is the problem with lies. The truth had to fight dirty to get out.

Casey waited for a response. "Can I help you?" she asked impatiently.

Amy blushed. "Um, Diego wants me to go with you to the soccer golf thing."

"Oh." Casey pursed her lips. "I...I was going to take my niece. Let me call her and tell her another time."

"No." Amy stopped Casey from picking up the phone. "I told Diego you probably had plans but he insisted." She stepped inside the office. "Bring her along. Please."

"She's ten and she never stops talking."

"I love kids." A chatty ten-year-old was the perfect way to keep her day around Casey intact.

"You sure?" Casey set the phone back down.

"Definitely. Let's do this."

An hour later Amy and Casey were racing down the 101 Highway with a jubilant ten-year-old in the backseat. Mia bounced to the pop tunes blaring from the radio. The second she had gotten into the car the mood transformed.

All the tension building between them dissipated like it had never existed.

"Oh. Turn that up, Aunt Casey."

"It's pretty loud already."

"But this is my favorite song." Mia drew the sentence out with a perfected pre-teen whine.

"You said the last one was your favorite song."

"It was until I heard this one."

Casey spun the dial on the radio the tiniest bit and chuckled. The laugh was one of the happiest, most genuine sounds Amy had heard in a while. She stole a glance at the woman beside her. Hands lightly gripped the steering wheel and her head slightly bobbing to the up-tempo beat. This Casey was as different from the woman of the last two days as day was from night. This was the real Casey.

"Sing, Mia. I know you know the words."

A second set of lyrics burst forth from the backseat, deeply out of tune, but full of so much joy that it didn't matter.

Casey turned toward Amy and with a broad smile and mouthed, "Sorry."

Amy caught her gaze just for a second before Casey turned back to the road. The blue of her eyes was luminous and no longer frozen. Her defensiveness had thawed for the moment. Amy wished that she'd been the one to trigger the change rather than the animated imp in the backseat. Mia belted out one song after another until Casey pulled into the parking lot at the golf course.

"We have reservations. I'll go check in."

"Have you ever played Footgolf?" Mia danced beside Amy as Casey talked with a lanky young man behind the counter of the pro shop.

"No. Have you?"

"Nope." She shrugged, and then grinned. "But I'm going to be pretty good. Coach chooses me for all the corner kicks," Mia said, with the true modesty of a ten-year-old.

"Oh, I better watch out then."

Amy heard Casey mention Diego's name, and the lanky man straighten up giving Casey his full attention. He couldn't get to the phone fast enough, and Casey turned to put up one finger to tell them it was going to be a minute.

"So what position do you play?" Amy asked, killing time.

"Forward, just like my Aunt Casey did."

Amy took in the casual way Casey was standing, light on her feet, aware of all the space around her. She held herself like an athlete.

Wait a second. Just like my Aunt Casey did? What happened to her? Amy realized that she knew nothing at all about Casey.

A man in a suit arrived at the pro shop. He came up to Casey and pumped her hand repeatedly, bowing his head a little as he did so. Amy felt the force of Diego's name from ten feet away.

"All right. We're good to go. Let's get our stuff." Casey headed back to them. The trunk of her Camry popped open with a satisfying *thunk,* and Casey yanked out a big blue-and-gold Bruin soccer duffel. Casey #3 was stitched across one side. A scuffed, but well-loved soccer ball was stuffed into a mesh side pocket. A couple more soccer balls rolled around loose in the trunk.

"Pick your weapon."

Amy chose a black and gold Adidas ball. Mia snapped up a neon pink one, and Casey grabbed a red one from out of the back.

"Shoes." Casey directed Mia to a backpack on the backseat. "You playing in those?" Casey frowned at Amy's tennis shoes.

Amy bit her lip. "Yeah, they're all I have. Hey, what about those turf shoes from yesterday?"

Casey unzipped a side pocket of the backpack and produced the shoes. "You mean these?"

Amy nodded.

"These are mine."

"What? You gave me your shoes yesterday?" Embarrassment warmed her cheeks. "Casey, you didn't have to do that."

"Actually, I did. That's my job. To pull shoes magically out of my bag whenever Diego needs them. Besides, I don't really use them that much anymore."

"I wouldn't have taken them if I had known."

"Where'd you think they came from?" Casey actually sounded like she wanted to know.

"I don't know. That wardrobe woman at the photo shoot or something. I don't know. I wasn't thinking. Look, it's okay. I'll just play in my sneakers." Amy shifted awkwardly. Her tennis shoes should have enough traction for her not to fall on her ass with the first kick. Casey nodded, unzipped the biggest compartment of the bag and pulled out a black graphite brace with two round hinges. It looked bionic. She fixed the brace around her knee with a few well-practiced tugs.

"ACL tear in my knee among other things." Casey shrugged as if it were no big deal. Amy had been around soccer long enough to know how dangerous knee injuries could be. A brace like this one usually signaled a career-ending injury. Casey's bag looked authentic. UCLA was a Division 1 school. Number two in the US college soccer rankings if she remembered correctly. Maybe Casey could shrug the injury off now, but at some point it had been a very big deal.

"Ready!" Mia bounded out the car with her turf shoes on. She grabbed Casey's arm and dragged her over to the green. However uncomfortable Amy had felt in the parking lot, it vanished as soon as they set their balls down on the first tee. Amy was ready to make fun of the game. Footgolf. The title alone was absurd.

The game consisted of eighteen holes carved out of the fairways of a regular golf course each ending in a cup the size of a garbage can. At first glance, Hole #1 looked deceptively simple. A straight par three that skirted through a bank of trees, it ended in a long narrow green. Mia couldn't wait to get started. She dropped her ball first, backed up for a running start and threw herself at it. The shot had a lovely lofting arc, and Amy knew why she was chosen for every corner kick. But this game demanded a driven ball, not height.

"Mia, get your body over the ball." Casey threw a sample kick in the air. Her body was bent as her foot came up with a snap. "You want distance not height."

"Got it. Can I go again?"

Casey looked to Amy for an answer.

"Sure. I don't care. We're not keeping score, are we?"

"You always need to keep score," Casey said, enigmatically. "Even if you tell no one." Amy wasn't sure they were talking about the game anymore. Casey turned to the fairway. She dropped her ball on the tee and kicked it in one fluid motion. Her shot sailed to the left of the trees and bounced down the fairway. The placement was perfect. Mia clapped her hands with delight. Excitement twinkled in Casey's eyes. "Your turn."

Amy stepped up to the tee and whispered to Mia, "So, I know you never played before, but your aunt's like a super-secret American Footgolf League star, right?"

"No, silly." Mia chortled. "This is the first time for her, too."

Amy carefully placed her ball and took note of the prevailing wind coming in from the ocean. She would have to favor the right to compensate for what two minutes ago was a delightful respite from the heat. Now that same breeze was her enemy. She took a deep breath, wound up the kick, and pulled the trigger. Her foot plowed into the ball with a sweet snap, sending it rising into the air. The shot dropped a good fifteen feet behind Casey's, but adrenalin zinged through her. She hadn't hauled out and kicked the stuffing out of a ball for over two years. Yesterday had been all about PR, and making Diego and the kids at the park look good. But today it was all about the simplicity of kicking a ball around the grass in the open air. Love for the game flooded through her.

"Not bad." Casey nodded.

The whack of another ball sounded behind them as Mia took her second shot.

"I did it! I did it. Come on."

Amy obediently trotted up the fairway after her.

"Come on, Aunt Casey," Mia called. "Last one there is a bag of poo."

"Nice. Where you get that one?" Casey loped after them favoring her bad knee.

"Dad."

"That's my brother," Casey said, as she breezed past Amy.

Within two holes the competition was as good as over. Casey parred the first and birdied the second, and had already grasped the secret to the putting game in Footgolf.

Amy's first instinct near the cup was to tap the ball in with inside of her foot. Just as she would've if they had been on a level soccer field. But this wasn't soccer, it was Footgolf and the greens undulated at the cup. Amy's putts wobbled around the hole as if the flag had a force field. She couldn't figure it out.

Casey, on the other hand, sank one putt after another. "How'd you do that, Aunt Casey?" Mia tugged at her aunt's sleeve and pulled her over to her own ball six feet from the cup.

"Like this. Put your foot on the ball."

Mia stomped on it as if she were killing a bug. "Easy. Pull your foot back, hips up." She dropped her hand on Mia's right hip and pushed the girl slightly forward. "Now slide your foot across. Don't come up on the ball. That'll make it bounce." Casey gave the girl a gentle push, and Mia sent the shot off toward the cup. It fell inside with a satisfying plunk.

"Yes!" She punched the air with her first.

At the next green Amy skimmed her foot across the ball but it hopped away from the cup like a rabbit.

"Help her," Mia ordered.

"Play down on the ball," Casey said, not moving an inch.

"No, go over there and help her." Mia pointed toward Amy.

Casey hesitated.

"I can figure it out," Amy said.

"She's not playing fair if she doesn't help you." Mia gave Casey a play kick in her behind to get her moving.

"The logic of a ten-year-old." Casey shrugged as she stepped up to Amy's side.

Just the nearness of her was enough to set Amy's heart beating. It thumped so loudly in her chest, she was sure that both Casey and Mia, and probably the father and son who were a hole behind, could all hear it. Casey laid a hand on Amy's hip with a touch so light Amy wasn't even sure that there was contact. But when she rolled the ball forward she felt a delicate push on her hip. The ball stayed true and fell into the cup. The hand was still at her hip. Amy willed the contact to linger.

"Nice shot." The praise was little more than a breath in her ear. It was all she could do to not fall back into full contact. Casey moved away first.

"Okay." Mia danced between them. "Now Aunt Casey can only kick with her left foot." When that didn't slow her down, Mia came up with a new restriction with every shot. "Close your eyes."

"Twirl around first."

"Do the Macarena."

Amy giggled at first, but by the hole number ten, she started laughing outright. They all did. At one point, when Casey had to neigh like a horse and gallop up to the ball, she actually snorted with unladylike laughter.

There was method to the madness. When they rolled into the pro-shop at the end of the round, Mia had beaten both of them soundly. "I win. I win," she sang.

"You sure did," Amy said. She deserved it, too. She had beaten them with her smarts when her skill wasn't enough.

The manager rushed out as soon as they came off the last green.

"Have fun?" he asked.

"Oh my God," Mia began. "I have never had as much fun in all my life."

Amy caught Casey's gaze and smiled. It had been a lot of fun.

"Well, I hope that you tell that to Mr. Torres. We would love to see him out here promoting our club and the sport."

"Of course." Casey turned serious.

"And if you could..." He glanced at Amy. "Hey! Aren't you... You're Amy Kimball, right?"

Amy blushed. This was the first time she had registered as a celebrity.

"You're Diego's fiancée," he said delightedly, and turned his back completely on Casey. "You can tell him. Tell him that this is the sport of the future and that he can be the first MLS star to..."

Amy stopped listening. Behind the man, Mia's impish grin had fallen right off her face. The girl looked first to Casey and then to Amy and then back to Casey. "Wait a sec," she said softly, and Amy strained to listen. "She's Diego's girlfriend? I thought... I mean... Aunt Casey aren't you and ...?"

Casey shook her head violently at her niece, and Mia questions skittered to a halt. Sadness along with disappointment flooded her young face. She opened her mouth again, but Casey's hand fell onto her shoulder and squeezed. Mia kept quiet.

The manager prattled on, but Amy's mind was reeling as she tried to get a handle on this new development. *Damn. Out of the mouth of babes.* Casey did have a thing for Diego. This whole situation was getting messier and messier.

"...next week. So maybe if he has a break from the Atoms, you and him could come back? Play a few holes on the house?"

Amy had no idea what he was talking about. "I'll ask him," she said, to shut him up. "I think we're leaving now."

Casey and Mia were halfway to the car. Casey had her arm draped across her niece's shoulder. They were engaged in a private conversation which came to a sudden halt as soon as Amy caught up with them. The drive back was a quiet one. No one said a word all the way down the freeway. Luckily, the traffic was light and the radio loud. Casey drove with a lead foot. They pulled into Diego's driveway in record time.

"It was really great to meet you," Amy said to Mia as she got out of the car.

"Me, too."

She looked at Casey but her face was turned away. She didn't need to see her eyes to know that the chill was back, and deeper than ever.

Amy stood listening to the scrunch of pebbles as Casey's car sped away. Behind her the front door opened with a click.

"Have a good time?" Tammy materialized beside her. She smiled a little too brightly, her lipstick matching the color of her hair exactly.

"I don't know." Amy tried not to let Tammy's sudden appearance unsettle her. Tammy seemed to be everywhere at once, keeping tabs. Amy let out the breath she had pretty much held all the way home in the car. She was done trying to figure out all these crazy people in Diego's household. She headed to where she should have gone in the first place.

"I'll be out by the pool if anyone needs me."

CHAPTER 6

AMY SLID HER PALMS DOWN the delicate fabric of her summer dress. The motion did nothing to wipe away the thin film of nervous sweat. They were outside Diego's parents' house and more than the heat was getting to her.

"You okay?" Diego asked.

"Little nervous," Amy admitted. "This one actually matters. Diego, if your family doesn't buy it, we're done."

"Relax. You've done great everywhere else."

"It doesn't bother you to lie to your own family?" Surely Diego couldn't compartmentalize his feelings so easily?

"Of course it does. But it is for their own good as well. When you get inside you'll see what my sacrifice has bought."

Yeah, but at what cost? It was a question that Diego didn't seem interested in, so she moved to one that interested her. "And your great-grandmother. How are we going to deal with her?"

"Yeah, Abuelita's a problem. But she only speaks Spanish, so she'll be my problem. Your challenge will be not eating too many of my mother's sweet banana empanadas. They're enough to destroy a man's training routine. Don't let me overindulge, okay? Or Rob will have my ass."

You wish. Amy bit her lip rather than have the words slip out. This whole evening would be an exercise in restraint. "You got the picture?"

"I do." He held up a padded manila envelope. Lucy Lewitt had messengered over two stills, a photoshopped one from the studio shoot and a more candid shot from the publicity stunt at the park. Diego had placed the doctored one on the mantel in his own den and had asked Casey to wrap the other one up as a festive little package.

"Are you sure it's not too early to give your mother a picture of us?"

"We're engaged, remember? Besides we'll only give it to her if things go well. Otherwise we'll just take it back home. No harm, no foul."

"Okay." Amy swiped her palms down her dress again.

Diego put his finger up on the doorbell. "Ready?"

"As I'll ever be."

He jabbed the button, and eight clear notes of a Westminster door chime rang loudly through the house.

"That's some door bell."

"High and low notes so Abuelita can hear it better. She's a little deaf."

The door swung open, and over a dozen people of all ages stood crammed into the pristine marble entry way. They all hooted and hollered their hellos. The marble on the floor and the soft taupe on the walls gleamed. The house looked so new it could have been built the day before.

"Coming through. Coming through." A handsome woman in her late forties pushed her way through the throng, shushing everyone around her as she went. She met Amy with an outstretched hand which quickly turned into a hug. "You're here at last. I'm Isabella, Diego's mom."

"Mrs. Torres. I'm so happy to meet you."

"Ah, call me Isabella. We're almost family now, right?"

Guilt surged in Amy. "Right."

"Let me see." Isabella lifted Amy's hand so the big diamond engagement ring shone in the afternoon sun. "Very nice, Diego, although I'm not sure I've forgiven you for keeping this secret from me."

Up close, the woman was more than handsome. She had high cheekbones and full lips. Diego had inherited her beauty.

"Amy, excuse this loco mob behind me," she said, and shooed everyone back to let them pass. "This is our family."

The noise started up again, as one older man, Diego's grandfather, pulled Amy into a big bear hug.

"Preciosa!" he said, over and over again as he passed her on to a plump woman by his side. His wife, Amy gathered.

The woman gripped Amy's chin with a thumb and forefinger and turned her face first one way and then the other.

"Que linda!" She nodded to her husband, her eyes flashing with merriment.

Amy was handed over to one relative after another until Diego pulled her to him protectively. "See I told you. You're already one of the family."

Amy wished she could copy Diego's nonchalance. Surely he must be feeling some conflict in this situation?

With an arm slung casually over her shoulder he led her into the great room. The furniture was modern and elegant, except for one overly ornate wooden chair. It was antique, obviously from Mexico, and held a place of honor at the far end of the room. On it perched one of the smallest women Amy had ever seen. Her snow-white hair was pulled back into a tight bun and a colorful traditional shawl covered her shoulders. She regarded Amy with a steady gaze which seemed to cut right into her.

Amy's smile died on her lips as soon as she saw her. This must be Abuelita. Amy resisted the urge to curtesy. Instead she stood quietly just inside the door.

The woman raised a heavily wrinkled hand and motioned her to come nearer. Amy looked to Diego who nodded an okay and gave her the tiniest of shoves forward.

Amy swallowed. She wasn't at all sure it was okay. The whole family had plunged into deathly silence, never a good sign. Abuelita raised a bony finger and placed it on Amy's shoulder.

"She wants you to turn around," Diego said; an unexpected tremor entered his voice which in turn sent nervous flutterings in Amy's chest. She spun a half-turn.

"And again." Diego added. Amy spun a second time until she was facing Abuelita once more. The woman's gaze dropped to her hips and lingered just long enough to make Amy truly uncomfortable.

"Le dara mucho hijos."

The family erupted into cheers of approval.

"What'd she say?" Amy leaned into Diego when the crowd thinned.

A blush crept onto his cheeks. "She said we'll make good babies."

Amy's stomach dropped. Now she was lying to an old woman whose only crime was wanting to see her great-grandson happy.

"Oh my God. Diego! You're on TV!" A teenage girl ran into the room. Diego's family moved en mass to the media room. Amy flinched as soon as she stepped through the door. An image of her face, as big as a billboard flashed on a huge screen at the far end. The laughter of the kids playing soccer with her and Diego at the park spilled out in to the family theater.

"She's got game," Marcus, Diego's old college coach and family friend announced and winked at her.

The TV piece was short but very effective. Even Amy liked them better as a couple after the show cut to commercial. Somewhere in the distance a door opened, and the delicious smell of meat roasting wafted in.

"A comer! Time to eat!" A male voice called out.

People began to move toward the backyard, sweeping Amy along with them. Someone thrust a frosty beer into her hand. Someone else handed her a plate and directed her to a table with so much food on it she was afraid the whole thing would collapse. Mounds of empanadas, tamales, meat still steaming from the grill, and a dozen other dishes she had never seen before took up every available space on the long table.

"You like carne asada?" Isabella pointed to the table.

"I don't know. There aren't a whole lot of good Mexican restaurants in rural Pennsylvania." She thrust her plate out to her hostess. "But I'm game. Load me up."

Isabella did just that and handed her a fork. The spicy, complex flavors of south of the border cooking flooded her mouth.

"It's delicious." It was the first truth she had uttered since she got there. As it turned out, it was that simple. A heartfelt compliment about the food, good childbearing hips, and several beers was all it took to bring Amy into Diego's family. At one point, she practically forgot it was all a ruse. Happiness flooded her. Even when her parents were alive, she had never had anything like this. Her family circle was too small. She reveled in the easy comradery that an afternoon surrounded by a huge family brought her. She could get used to this, and she had to remind herself this wasn't her real life. She was at work.

As the afternoon came to a close, Amy jumped up with the other women to clear the dishes. The Torres kitchen was huge. Like every other room in the house, it was filled with the latest conveniences. Amy already knew that Diego bought this house for his family before he had bought his own. No wonder the weight of the world was on his shoulders. The American dream was a heavy load for anyone to carry, especially a gay, Mexican soccer star.

Isabella took the dishes from Amy and directed her to a couch in a quiet corner. "He seems a lot happier, maybe calmer, since he's been with you." She sat beside her.

Amy bit her lip. She didn't want to lie to this woman who had welcomed her with open arms. She chose her words carefully so she wouldn't have to. "It's been really good for both of us."

Something dark flitted across Isabella's face but was gone almost immediately. Amy steadied herself for the inevitable warning she was sure was coming. Do right by Diego or else! Of course, she didn't want to hear it. Tammy had said the same thing enough times for everyone. Amy took a deep breath. Hearing Diego's mother out was her penance for lying to such a wonderful family.

"Be careful, mija." A sad smile played at Isabella's lips. "My boy's a good man. But I'm afraid he may not know himself."

What did that mean? Amy searched Isabella's face for an explanation. Did Isabella know about Diego? The dark eyes which were so similar to her son's gave nothing more away.

Diego appeared at her elbow and saved Amy from responding. "You two are thick as thieves." He slid an arm around Amy's waist and playfully scowled at his mother. "You're not telling her all my secrets, are you?"

Isabella chuckled and reached over to ruffle her son's hair. "No, of course not."

It all seemed so very natural. Amy looked from mother to son. Apparently Diego wasn't the only actor in the family.

"Mama." Diego produced the wrapped picture from behind his back. "This is for you." He then slid a glance at Amy as if to say, *See, I told you it would go well.*

Isabella laughed and opened up the wrapping paper. "I love presents."

"It's only something small," Diego said.

Isabella slid the picture of the happy couple into the open. Head down, she examined it intently for a long moment. So long that Amy grew anxious. So long that Diego finally reached over and pointed to a kid in the background. "That's Mario Duenas, Maria del Carmen's grandson."

"Is it? My, he's a big boy now." Her gaze was still fixed on the photograph.

"And a good player." Now Diego was beginning to sound anxious.

"Thank you for this, mijo." His worried tone jolted her into giving him a quick hug. "And you too, Amy." She turned to Amy. Isabella's look spoke volumes.

She did know.

Amy tucked her hair into the back of her dress and pressed herself into the soft leather seat of Diego's vintage Mustang convertible. She'd always thought she would like convertibles, but the stiff breeze whipped around the windshield and tangled her long hair. Thanks to the heatwave, the night hadn't cooled yet. Sweat prickled her back and mixed uncomfortably with her hair. A hair shirt. The penance seemed appropriate.

"Thank you for that. I think it went well." Diego seemed immune to both Amy's and his mother's discomfort. Amy bit the inside of her bottom lip. Should she or shouldn't she tell him?

She could hear Paul Knight shouting inside her head, *Mind your own goddamn business!*

Diego should know, she decided. He might even be happier for it, especially if he could live his life the way he wanted to, openly and without remorse. She turned toward him so her words would not be cut off by the wind. "I think your mother knows."

"Knows what?" Diego asked.

"About you. And probably about us, too."

Diego clenched the steering wheel until his knuckles went white and kept his eyes straight on the road ahead.

"No. She doesn't," he said finally, shifting the car into a lower gear to take the corner hard and fast.

Amy fixed her gaze on him. His expression had hardened. Denial oozed from every pore.

"I think—"

"There's nothing to think or know. I'm not doing anything with anybody except you. And as we both know, that's not really anything either."

"Okay." Amy got the message and dropped the subject. If her boss didn't want to talk about the elephant in the room, then they wouldn't. They drove on in silence. How was she going to repair this?

"Your parents' house is lovely," she said.

No answer.

"The food was really good."

Diego sighed. "Mm."

Not an actual word, but at least she was making a little bit of progress. Amy turned the pages of the afternoon over in her mind so she could put even more distance between them and the one topic that Diego wouldn't acknowledge.

"I really liked your old coach. The one from UCLA. What was his name?"

Amy knew his name, but she needed an answer from Diego.

"Marcus."

"It's great that you've stayed in touch with him."

"He's a great guy." A little bit of warmth crept into Diego's voice. Not for her, but she would take whatever she could get at this point. "He's always got my back."

"How?"

"He found Casey for me."

Amy's stomach lurched. She absolutely shouldn't bite. Two dangerous conversations in a row were two too many, and the minefields buried in this one were much harder to detect. She tried to beat down the curiosity rising in waves and actually opened her mouth to ask something about his great-grandmother. Instead, she heard herself say, "What do you mean found?"

"Marcus is involved with the woman's program at UCLA. He knew Casey when she played there."

The blue and gold Bruin soccer bag popped into Amy's mind, and the puzzle pieces of Casey's history started to slip together.

"She played there?" Amy echoed back.

"Yeah. She was the real deal too, until she blew out her knee."

"I saw the brace." What was wrong with her? She couldn't stop herself talking about Casey. "I didn't know they even made braces that big. It's like a leg from the Iron Man costume."

"You don't even know the half of it. It was a terrible injury. And to make it all worse, she had just been called up to the women's national team."

"You're kidding." There wasn't a girl alive who seriously kicked a ball down a soccer field and hadn't dreamed about such a call.

"Not even a little bit. Got the call at the UCLA soccer office. Marcus actually picked up the phone. It was wild. Nobody expected it. You see, she was off their radar. She hadn't come up through their youth program where they usually get their players. So she must have been amazing."

"So what happened?"

"Casey did. UCLA had a summer scrimmage. Marcus told her not play, but Casey's as loyal as a dog and she wasn't going to leave her teammates high and dry."

Amy sighed; she didn't really need another reason to like Casey any more.

"I think it was the goalie from the other team who took her out. And that was it." Diego smacked the steering wheel in frustration. "She tried to come back. The national team was even willing to give her another tryout. They're pretty forgiving that way, but the knee was never the same."

"Man. That's tough."

"You're telling me. She would've made it too. That makes it far worse."

"So you gave her a job?"

"Marcus wanted her to start coaching once she graduated. Had even talked to UCLA, I think. She turned him down flat. Said it would be too hard to watch other players doing what she couldn't anymore. So yeah, I gave her a job. I needed an assistant. She understood soccer, and she's super smart. It was weird at first, and sometimes still is. But I seem to specialize in weird relationships and making them work." He threw her a smile.

"Yes, I know." She smiled back and blew out a breath of relief. She filed away the helpful fact that soccer cured all ills with Diego.

"I'm not sure her heart's in the job, though. I mean how could it be? She was pre-med at UCLA. Finished all her courses while she was rehabbing. And now she's an assistant?"

"There are a lot of reasons why people take jobs," Amy said, thinking of her own experience at the Valley Arms.

"Hey, maybe you could get to know her. Become friends and find out if she's happy or not? You think you could do that?"

"I could try. But I'm not sure she likes me much."

"I heard her telling Tammy that you were great with her niece or cousin or somebody."

"Her niece. Mia."

"Yeah, that's right. Her niece. Try to find out if she's happy, would you? I don't want to hold her back or anything."

"I'll see what I can find out." Amy turned her gaze onto the road speeding by outside. The yellow dashes on the street blurred into one big line. No wonder there was an edge to Casey. Slapped down on the way to the national team. Life wasn't fair, as Amy realized all too well. But still... Hadn't her boss just given her a new assignment? She was being paid to do this job, and now the position included getting to know Casey. How could she say no to her employer?

"Oh, before I forget. Paul texted. He wants to talk to you about something at Caffeine Cowabunga tomorrow. He'll pick you up at ten?"

"Sure." Damn. Not being able to say no to your boss was a double edged sword.

It's easy for Diego, Atoms superstar forward, to juggle soccer and the love of his life, Amy Kimball. Life for them is a ball. #Amiego.

Knight showed her the Twitter feed off his phone.

120

"Hashtag Amiego? Who thought that up?" Amy said.

"Lucy, of course. I think we may be overusing the ball metaphor, but it's still great publicity," Knight answered.

"Don't you think everyone's spreading it on a little thick? What's going to happen when we actually don't get married?"

"We'll cross that bridge later." Knight handed her the phone again. There was a picture of her and Diego from the studio shoot splashed across it. "You guys look good."

They did. Really good. Amy and Diego juggled the ball around the studio, but where the green screen had been there was now a gorgeous soccer field with snow covered mountains way in the background.

"Where are we supposed to be?" asked Amy.

"The land of true love."

"So it's just as fake as our relationship?"

"Shush! Someone will hear you."

"No one's listening."

And it was true. Knight couldn't have chosen a more ridiculous place for their meeting. Caffeine Cowabunga was a restaurant, a coffee house, and a surf shop all rolled into one, about twenty-five miles from the ocean. The coffee house rambled over a wooden deck close to a bubbling creek. Amy was pretty sure the creek was the only thing that reached the ocean from there. The surf shop catered to rich kids from the Valley who fancied themselves surfers, but Amy would have bet hard money that only a few of them ever made it to the beach with a board.

"You want a latte? I want a latte." Knight called the waitress over without waiting for Amy's answer.

"Hey, what's going on with Simon?" Amy asked, wondering why they were here. Knight could have just e-mailed her the picture.

"He just booked his first gig at the Roadhouse in a couple of weeks, I think."

"Really?" Amy frowned. Simon still hadn't answered one of her texts. But she had no desire to admit that to Knight of all people

"He has no idea you set this all up, does he?"

"I'm sure you didn't bring me here to tell me how to run my friendship with Simon."

"No, I didn't. But I'll messenger over a couple of tickets to the show. You go if you want. Congratulate him in person. Bring Diego even. You two need more dates that seem organic and not a publicity stunt." He took the phone back. "I'll send a plant to take some pictures. Get them onto Facebook."

Amy sighed. Count on Knight to take the one non-selfish thing she had done in a long time and turn it to his advantage.

"Why exactly are we here?" Amy asked.

He pulled a manila envelope with the Horowitz and Kane logo embossed on it from his briefcase and slid it across the table, keeping his palm flat on it.

"We're all pretty happy with the way things are going. You know Diego told me that..." And here Knight lowered his voice to barely a whisper. "...if he wanted a girlfriend he would want it to be you."

"Thanks, I guess." A faint blush crept into her cheeks.

"Don't go developing real feelings for him."

"I'm not. Give me some credit here." How could she tell Knight that when she fell asleep at night she dreamed about cool blue eyes and not warm brown ones, even if the owner of the blue eyes hadn't said one word to her in the last two days.

"We haven't told you the whole story."

Here it was. "Why doesn't that surprise me?" Amy marveled at the fact that in the wacky, mixed-up world she was living in, this creepy man was the only one she could speak to without measuring her words first.

"The situation," Knight said, ignoring Amy's sarcasm, "is much more complicated than we've led you to believe."

"Again, not surprised."

"Before I go any further, you need to remember that you're under a confidentially contract that extends to this conversation as well."

Despite herself, Amy tilted her head waiting for Knight to continue. When he didn't, she said,

"How can I forget. It seems to be your catch phrase."

"Good. So the whole crazy idea of inserting you into Diego's life came about because of these." He tapped the manila envelope with his fingers. "A couple of months ago, we got the first one." He lifted his hand. "Please look at them, but be discreet."

"Okay." Amy had no idea what to expect. She dropped the envelope to her lap. It was stuffed with photographs. She slid the first one out.

"Shit," she said, softly.

"Yeah. Not good. Not good at all."

She slid the picture out an inch more to make sure she had seen it correctly. Diego, gorgeous in a teal shirt, was kissing a man on the cheek. In another, he had his arms looped around two handsome men outside the soccer stadium. She flipped through the rest of the pictures. They were all of Diego with different men, at the beach, on a boat, even by his own pool, and not one snapshot left his sexual preference in doubt. Amy's stomach sank. She'd actually begun to enjoy her role as Diego's girl, but if any of these pictures were made public, it would end all that. What's more, she had actually believed Diego when he had told her there was no one in his life, and that he would do nothing to jeopardize his family's happiness. Obviously, that didn't include taking up with any Tom, Dick, or Harry that came his way.

"How could he be so stupid?" Amy asked. Was this why he was so nonchalant at his parents' house? Mr. Nice Guy was just an act, and he was playing everyone. She was the stupid one, it seemed.

"Well, that's the odd part. He claims he wasn't."

"Of course, he would. He got caught with his hand in the cookie jar. What else would he say?" The bitterness in her voice surprised her. She had trusted Diego. She shoved the photos back in the envelope.

"That's what I thought, too. We all did. But he says that he doesn't know any of these men. He's never seen any of them before in his life."

"I would say he's lying."

"At first glance, yes. But we had an expert at the firm examine them, and all of them are photoshopped," Knight said. "Not one of these is real. Diego's telling the truth."

"What firm? Horowitz and Kane?"

"Yeah. They have all sorts of people there." Knight dismissed the question. He wrapped both hands around his coffee and leaned towards her conspiratorially. "You see, a couple of months ago, Horowitz got the first picture. And we've been getting one nearly every week since."

"Blackmail?"

Knight shrugged. "So far there's been no demands. Just the pictures."

"So it's not blackmail?" Amy was surprised.

"No. At least, not yet. Creating a picture like this is not illegal. And we can't go to the police because there's no extortion. We tried to figure out where they're coming from, but the firm's investigator drew a blank on that, too. Except that whoever it is, they're not getting the pictures off the internet. There's got to be an inside source. So basically, we got nothing to go on, so far." He squeezed the coffee cup so tightly, Amy wondered if it might shatter. She leaned back in her seat.

"And you're worried that this crazy, who enjoys playing with pictures of Diego, will do something worse than demand money? Is that it?"

Knight threw Amy a grateful look. "Yes. That's it exactly. All it takes is one of these, just one, posted to the internet. And it doesn't matter if it's fake, Diego's endorsement deals will dry up. Gay men don't sell shit in the Latino market."

She didn't like Knight. She was pretty sure she never would. She just couldn't get past that creepy vibe. But the worried tone in his voice, the care with the envelope, it wasn't just his usual dramatics. He had real affection for Diego.

"I get it. The pictures are why he was playing so badly and why we had to rush into our engagement."

"Yes." Knight scowled. "If the truth ever got out, we, well I, thought we could hide it with a lie. And if we got our lie out there first..."

Amy nodded her head. In this day and age of social media, his crazy plan made perfect sense. "But that's not why you brought me here. To tell me all this."

"No. We want you to take on something else for us," he said.

Amy closed her eyes and sighed. She was feeling sorry for Diego, and maybe even for Knight, just the tiniest little bit, but she was in deep enough. "What?" she asked curtly.

"Last week the pictures changed from cute vacation photos to this." He pulled a second envelope from his briefcase. "Prepare yourself." He passed the envelope over.

"Oh my God!" Diego still had a starring role. This time, however, there was nothing left to the imagination. "These aren't real either, are they?"

"No, but this is gay porn. We're in a different league now, as you can see. It's imperative we find out who is responsible."

"So now you want me to be a fake detective as well as a fake girlfriend?"

"Yes." Knight didn't hear her sarcasm. "We think it's someone close to him. Probably someone who has access to the house. We want you to keep your ears and eyes open. Just look around and see what you can find out."

"I don't know. Whoever it is seems like a real nut job."

"Look, if we can ID this person, we get them out of Diego's life."

Amy pursed her lips and said nothing.

"I hear from the grapevine that the national team is sniffing around. This would be the absolute worst time for anything like this to break. You owe it to him."

Knight was wrong. She didn't owe Diego anything. But she did like the man, and if she could help him chase his dream, then she should.

"Okay. I'll help. Unless it gets too weird."

"It won't. You're just looking around. That's it." Knight grinned. "Oh, and you can't tell Diego. He doesn't know anything about the turn this has taken."

"I don't like lying to him," she said. Although she seemed to be lying to everyone else, lately.

"We'll make it worth your while. Remember, this is your job."

Amy rolled her eyes. "No shit, Sherlock." She went back to disliking him. "You know, at some point, you're not going to be able to buy me."

Knight smiled again. Now she was speaking his language. He grabbed his briefcase, popped it open and dug around. Finally, he pulled out a set of round, black keys. He dangled them over the table in front of Amy's face. "Let me know when we get to that point."

"Please tell me those aren't car keys?"

"You betcha. To a little beauty parked right outside in the lot." He gave a smug smile.

"You have got to be kidding. I'm not taking a car." A jolt of anger hit her, and heat flooded her face. "Especially from you." The last three words sounded harsh even to her ears, but she was sick and tired of Knight assuming money solved all problems.

Knight shrugged off the insult easily. "Actually, it was Diego's idea. He's worried about you driving around in that deathtrap of yours."

Amy took a deep breath and tried to shove the anger away. Diego only meant kindness with the gesture.

"He needs to know that you'll be safe on the road, show up to events when you need to. And there's an image to maintain as well."

They had her there. Her car was definitely on its last wheel. A hard slam of the driver's door and the back bumper could hit the ground. And then there was that horrible rattle whenever she shifted into second gear.

"Look, we're not giving the car to you. It still belongs to Horowitz and Kane. But you can have the use of it while you're on the job. Consider it one of the perks of hashtag Amiego." He shook the keys seductively. "It comes with insurance."

The alarm bells she'd heard when she'd met him outside of Starbucks clanged loudly again. Accepting the car keys would kill her a little bit more on the inside, but she told herself she had to do her job. Amy reached out to grab the keys.

"That's a good girl," Knight said, as her fingers closed around the key fob.

Amy sighed. It sure didn't feel good.

Knight made her swear again that she wouldn't tell Diego about the latest pictures, dropped some cash on the table, and walked away without looking back. Amy lifted the bills to see that Knight had left only a dollar tip. She added two more bills to the pile. Two dollars wouldn't change a life, but it was the principle of it. She picked up the car keys with a slightly freer heart.

When she stepped out into the parking lot, she realized that Knight hadn't actually told her which car was on loan to her. Huge SUVs and luxury sedans filled the spaces. Any one of which would instantly turn her into a soccer mom the second she opened the door. Shame whipped around her. Maybe Knight was right and everyone was driven by greed. It had only taken her a few seconds and already she was looking this gift horse deep in the mouth.

She pressed the button on the key and a corresponding beep came from behind a huge Cadillac Escalade. She skirted the Cadillac to see an adorable Mini-Cooper convertible roadster. She circled the car. Sexy carbon black stripes ran down the white hood, while both rear view mirrors popped with the same deep black. She opened the door and sank into the front seat. Inside she fingered the red trim and slid her hand over the dash. Everything about the car screamed luxury. She rested her head against the leather headrest. Did all deals with the Devil come with cars this nice? Metaphorically they must. That's why they were so painless to broker.

Amy slipped the key in the ignition. The turbo-charged engine roared then relaxed. The sexy rumble dampened some of her misgivings, and she eased out of the parking space and onto the road of no return.

CHAPTER 7

Slender arms wrapped Amy in a welcoming hug. Cyndy, the Irish pop star and wife of Scotty Westerman, the Atoms latest international purchase, gave Amy the same glamorous smile that graced teen magazines all over the world. She led her to a seat at the front of the Atoms' private box high on the fifty-yard line.

"Tread lightly," she murmured for Amy's ears only. "The real game's played here."

The other girlfriends and wives immediately gathered, sniffing around her like a new hound at the dog park. Cyndy kept a protective arm around the back of her chair to ward off the more aggressive women from snagging a seat nearby. Amy's position was tenuous. Diego raked in one hundred and fifty times more in salary than their men did for running around the same field playing the same game. And that didn't even include the endorsements. A lot of these couples were living hand to mouth on the low MLS minimum salary, and the inequity of their positions with that of Amy and Cyndy swirled around the luxury box on this balmy night like a summer storm.

Amy immediately saw the way it was. She looked around making eye contact with the nearest women.

"I can't believe all this. You know, during the pre-season I was pulling drafts at the Valley Arms and watching all this on TV. And now... Now I'm here." Her delighted laugh was genuine and came through loud and clear, and most of the women lowered their hackles. Cyndy gave her shoulder a little squeeze; Amy was initiated into the pack.

In truth, Diego had already done all the heavy lifting before she had even got there. He had never forgotten what it was like to be a penniless rookie. So now that he had made it big, he routinely invited their husbands out for meals, shared his bounty from Adidas, and never took on airs. Thanks to Diego, the women were primed to like her. Amy's actual enthusiasm for the game—and, more importantly, her knowledge of the players she had watched on the Valley Arm's big screen—put her firmly in favor. It didn't hurt that the Atoms were having a great game against the New England Riot. At the end of the first half, the Riot's best player streaked toward the goal and the Atoms' sweeper moved in to block his shot. A very pregnant redhead at the far end of the luxury box lumbered up to cheer the play.

"That's her husband," Cyndy said by way of explanation.

After the halftime break, the team trotted back onto the field with a certain jauntiness to their step. They took it straight to the Riot. Diego timed his run perfectly. Scotty served up a beautiful pass and Diego burst into the opposition's penalty area with the ball at his feet. His shot came hard and fast. The Riot's goalie didn't stand a chance.

Amy rose with the rest of the stadium, pumping her fist in the air for the hometown hero. She looked down at Cyndy, who still sat in her seat and shouted over the crowd. "What a pass from Scotty. Oh my goodness. That was amazing."

Cyndy smiled. "Thanks. Who knows how many of those he has left in him," she said, wistfully.

After the game, the women waited for their men in the corridor by the locker rooms. Spirits soared. The Atoms had won 2-0. Diego charged through the door with a wide grin and grabbed Amy, lifting her and spinning her around.

"Great game!" Amy laughed, and then since her new best friends were watching, she laid a wet one on Diego. The two glasses of wine she'd had back in the luxury box gave the kiss a natural touch. The pregnant redhead let out a soft "ahh," and Cyndy punched Scotty playfully on the shoulder.

"Remember when we used to be like that?" she said.

"Aye. Sure we still are." He grabbed Cyndy and dipped her into a swooning kiss. Everyone hooted their approval. Diego dropped Amy lightly to the ground. Smiles and laughs greeted her at every turn. She had to remind herself that this was just another day at the office.

"You ready to go?" Diego asked.

"Just a second." She found Cyndy and gave her a quick hug. "Thank you," she whispered. Amy wasn't a fool; she knew that even with Diego's generosity she wouldn't have had a chance with these women unless Cyndy had given her the seal of approval.

Cyndy cupped her cheek with one hand. This close, Amy could see the tiny age lines around the older woman's face as Cyndy smiled at her. "My pleasure, honey."

"Mine, too." Who would have guessed that she would actually like this woman? As a teenager, with her nose always deep in a book, Amy had looked down on pop figures like Cyndy. But the warm strength in Cyndy's eyes told the story of a woman who was sure of her place in the world and didn't view other people's successes as her failures.

"Oh, you must come to Stephanie's baby shower tomorrow afternoon." Cyndy glanced the group behind her. "Right, Steph?"

"Yes, please do." Stephanie, the redhead, cradled her baby bump with both hands.

"I'd love to." Amy grinned over at Diego.

"Great. See you then. We'll text you the info." Cyndy said and grabbed her husband by the hand. "Honey we need to get home. You know Danny won't go to sleep until he sees you."

"The bairns. They rule the roost." Scotty shook his head and dutifully followed his wife to the players' parking lot.

It wasn't until after her morning run the next day that Amy realized Cyndy didn't have her contact info. She could ask Diego for a text number, but the rhythmic metal clanking from downstairs told her that it was a fitness day. Diego took Rob's training sessions very seriously. Disturbing him wasn't a good idea. She could ask Casey, but she had seen neither hide nor hair of her over the last few days. Maybe this was her in?

Tiny flutters of excitement ran through her chest. She now had an excuse to seek out Casey. Without really admitting it to herself, she had been looking for one for days.

"What do you think?" she asked Dulce. "It's as good an excuse to talk to her as any." Dulce thumped her tail on the wooden floor and groaned in her sweet little way as Amy rubbed her belly with one foot. "Yes, that goes without saying. I gotta dress the part."

Amy slid the hangers over until she landed on what she wanted. She fingered the lightweight material of the bathing suit. "Too much?" Dulce nipped her ankle. "I know. But I stupidly bought it. I might as well see if it works."

A few minutes later Amy stood admiring herself in the full-length bathroom mirror. White board shorts with large black hibiscus flowers hugged her hips and thighs. She turned one way and then another and grinned at the view of her behind. If only Lucy Lewitt could see her now. The simple black bikini top with its discreet underwire held everything up top in place, but barely. She slid the silver V, which held the two cups together and was the designer's trademark, right into the space between her breasts. The V subtly focused all attention onto her cleavage. The designer was a very clever man.

The outfit had been an impulse buy at Caffeine Cowabunga when Knight was late for one of their meetings. Amy had nearly flung it back at the disinterested salesman when he had told her the outrageous price for something that covered so little of her body. Now, with her breasts thrust up so full and curvy that she hardly recognized them as her own, she would have paid twice the price.

Dulce danced around her feet. "Look," Amy told her. "We're color-coordinated, you and me. Ready to rumble?"

Amy flipped on the misters before she stepped outside. Still in the clutches of a heatwave that wouldn't break, outside felt as hot as the Sahara. The heat rolled off the flagstone in waves, and now little drops of water shot out from the patio roof, instantly cooling the air before it dropped onto her heated skin. She positioned one of Diego's plush lounge chairs in the direction of the side gate. Casey parked on the garage side of the house, and Amy would be right in her path as she came into work. She would have to acknowledge her. Also, this way Amy would hear the Camry as it scrunched over the pebbled driveway and would have plenty of time to pose to give Casey a clear view of the silver V clasp and what lay on either side. Not that anything would come of it. Casey wasn't buying, and even if she were, Amy couldn't really sell what she was plating up. She sighed at the futility of the entire exercise. If she had any sense, she'd get up and go back inside.

Instead, she opened the trashy mystery she was reading. Her bedside table was crammed with books she never had the time to read while holding down two full-time jobs. Amy sank back in the lounger and read until her eyelids began to droop with the heat. She closed her eyes and dropped the book to her chest. The cool spray from the misters settled on her skin, soft as a caress. She relaxed into a daydream, allowing her mind to take her to dark, dirty, and thoroughly sexy places. Casey's breasts in a translucent wet T-shirt flashed into focus. Nice, really nice. But Casey just standing there doing nothing wasn't going to cut it in this fantasy.

In her daydream, Casey entered by the side gate. She was wearing the wet T-shirt from their first encounter by the pool. The T-shirt clung to her body like a glove, hugging her firm breasts. Longing spread from the pit of Amy's stomach and tingled along her thighs. Casey came to a halt beside the lounger; desire burned in her eyes.

"Careful of the sun," she said. "You look a little red around the shoulders."

Amy picked up the sunblock. "It's SPF 50. It should work."

"Maybe you missed a spot."

"Maybe. Can you get it for me?"

"Maybe I can." Within seconds strong hands swept across Amy's skin, rubbing lotion onto her shoulders with broad sweeping stokes. Then the touch turned delicate and dropped down toward the swell of her breasts. Amy groaned softly, whether in the fantasy or in real life she couldn't tell. Tentatively, Casey slid the straps of the bikini top off her shoulders. Her hands slid over Amy's soft flesh to tug at the silver V and loosen the clasp. Casey slipped her fingers under the fabric and stroked Amy's tightened nipples. She circled and caressed until Amy moaned, and then she squeezed hard sending shivers all the way down her body. Amy arched her back.

"Are you okay?" Casey asked.

"Um," she sighed. "More than okay." Abruptly she realized the question hadn't come from her fantasy world. She opened her eyes. The bright sunlight was harsh even behind her sunglasses. For a moment, all she could see were bright sun flares. Slowly, Casey came into focus. She wore skimpy red shorts with a tight tank-top. She looked great, super sexy great. The real Casey with her hot lean body trumped fantasy Casey any day. Until she met that frosty stare.

"Seriously, you okay? You look spaced out, and you've dropped your book."

Amy wished the big, comfy lounge cushion would unzip and swallow her whole. She had been waiting for days to run into Casey, and fate delivered her at this exact moment?

"I must have fallen asleep." She rushed into the lie before she realized how lame it was. She could feel the heat spread to her entire face.

Casey bent down to pick up the book. Lovely, lean muscles ran all the way to her shoulder. Amy filed that particular detail away for her next fantasy. Casey looked at the cover as she handed the book back to her. "Oh, I like this series."

"Me too."

Their fingers brushed sending little sparks up Amy's arm. *Is she feeling this, too?* Casey didn't release the book, maintaining the touch. Their eyes met. Casey's were full of question. Was it the same question as Amy's, "Are you feeling this?" They stood like that for a couple of heartbeats, and then Casey dropped her hold on the book.

"Enjoy," she said, indicating the paperback. "I got to get back to work. Diego leaves for Chicago tomorrow, and I have a million things to do." A slight flush crept into Casey's cheeks. "Sorry. I mean, I know you know he's going out of town. Away game and all that. It's just that I'm always busy with stuff before he goes."

Amy titled her head. Did Casey seem a little flustered?

"Go ahead," she said, when all she wanted was for her to stay. Casey took a step toward the pool house and then turned back. Amy's heart missed a beat. She desperately wanted to pat the empty space next to her and say, "Sit down."

"Oh, I almost forgot. Cyndy Westerman's assistant sent a text this morning with an address for you. Should I send it to you?" The composure was back in her voice, and her face had returned to its natural color.

"Yes, please." Amy watched her walk away across the flagstones. She almost glided, her walk was so athletic. Amy eyes wandered down to her behind, so tight and cute in those clingy shorts. Amy bit her lip and forced her gaze down to the book in her hand. These fantasies about Casey were making things worse for her. She needed to concentrate on the fake relationship that was paying her bills and forget about the other fake relationship that was giving her nothing but headaches.

The Mini-Cooper sprinted around the bends as Amy drove high into the hills above Glendale. Stephanie's house was the next valley over, and Amy said a heartfelt thank you to Horowitz and Kane for not skimping on the extras with this car. She would have already lost her way half a dozen times without the built-in GPS. What she really needed, though, was a navigation device for her life. Why was she turning toward Casey at every chance when she should be heading in a different direction entirely? There had been other women who had flirted with her since Darla at Penn. That handsome, butch film editor who had come into the coffee house and had tried to buy her coffee at the end of her shift. The adorable blonde at the track who had run with her for weeks before giving up. None of them had touched her the way Casey had. Or maybe it wasn't Casey at all. Maybe it was everything?

Since her parents' deaths, she had compartmentalized all her emotions, not just her romantic ones. Could they be bubbling to the surface now because they couldn't be contained any longer? Perhaps it was because she wasn't racing from job to job and finally had the time to slow down and think about things? Plus, she had to admit, Casey was an easy distraction from life and all its problems. No. That was over simplifying the matter. She suspected it was really because she knew Casey had feelings for

Diego. Casey wasn't gay and that made her a safety net for Amy's sad little escapist fantasies.

"Your destination is on the right." The GPS interrupted her pointless reflections.

Amy pulled up before a traditional California ranch house laid out on one level. An open wooden fence ran the length of the lawn. Pink balloons were tied to the mailbox, and a huge "IT'S A GIRL" banner hung in the lounge window. Stephanie greeted Amy at the door with a smile and a quick hug.

"Your home is lovely," Amy said, handing her the gift-wrapped children books she had picked up on the way over.

"Oh, this is my sister's house. Brandon and I live in an apartment closer to the stadium. It's not as nice as this," Steph said lightly, as if it didn't matter, but Amy was again reminded of the inequity between the players' wages. "Come out to the back. That's where everyone is."

Atoms' wives and girlfriends and many people Amy didn't recognize were crammed onto the brick patio and small green lawn. Cyndy saw her as soon as she stepped out into the grass and waved her over.

"Yoo-hoo, honey. Over here. Come join us." Amy joined the small group sitting under a pergola, heavy with purple wisteria.

"It's like twenty degrees cooler over here in the shade." Karla, the goalkeeper's wife, scooted over to make room.

Cyndy jumped up to give Amy a quick continental kiss on both cheeks. "This whole shindig seemed like a much better idea when I RSVP'd in the cool air conditioning of my house. It never gets this hot back home."

"It used to never get this hot here." Karla laughed and wiped her brow for effect.

"Suck it up, ladies. It always heats up right around the play-offs," said another woman whose name Amy had forgotten.

"Let's hope you're talking about more than the weather." Cyndy said. "I'm not sure how many more seasons Scotty has in him. I'd like to see him go out on top."

"From your lips, Cyndy. From your lips."

A woman who looked so like Stephanie it had to be her sister appeared at the edge of the lawn. "Ladies, there's cake and games inside. Follow me."

Amy had never been to a baby shower before. Her friends just weren't in that stage of life, and she didn't know what to expect when Stephanie's sister led her little group into the den. Certainly not the games that followed. Ten opened newborn diapers sat on the coffee table, full of dark gooey stuff.

"What's that?" Amy was appalled.

"Chocolate. Why? What'd you think?" Cyndy laughed. "Oh, sweetie, I forget how young you are." Amy bristled. "Don't be mad. I'd give my right arm to be offended if someone told me I was too young," Cyndy said. "I spent most of my early twenties and all of my teens trying to act older than I was." A wistful look came into her eyes. "Enjoy it while you can, because believe me, it passes too soon. Come on. Let's play." Cyndy picked up the diaper closest to her and brought the gooey mess up to her nose. "Mint crème!"

She handed the diaper to Amy. "Give it a shot, but I'm warning you, I'm pretty good at this game."

"What do I do?"

"Smell it, and see if you can tell what the flavor the dirty nappy is."

"Okay." Amy put her nose close to the mess. She wasn't entirely sure that she wasn't being played for a fool.

"You're right, it's mint crème." Her eyes narrowed in challenge. "I'm going to give you a run for your money."

"Game on."

They went diaper for diaper. Milk chocolate, peanut butter, caramel, dark chocolate, coffee chocolate. Amy identified each one easily until they got to the last one. The dark and familiar scent stumped Amy until the last second when she pulled the answer out of her hat. "Hershey's syrup!"

"She's right," Stephanie's sister said.

"I've met my match." Cyndy conceded defeat.

"Young nose." Amy laughed. "And I'm American."

"You got me on both accounts."

The other games ran the gamut from guessing the names of the baby to decorating newborn onesies with fabric paint. Finally, all played out, Stephanie's guests plopped down on the sectional sofa in the den and grabbed a cupcake from a tray on the coffee table.

"Careful, ladies. One of these cupcakes contains a surprise. Hope you're the winner."

"What's the surprise?" Amy turned to Cyndy.

"Just eat it gingerly. You'll know it if you bite down on it."

Amused, she bit down into the center of her cupcake into something hard. "What the hell?" She fished around in her mouth and pulled out a tiny plastic baby.

"Amy got it!" Cyndy pointed a finger at the chocolate covered baby on Amy's palm.

"I did. What'd I win?"

The whole group broke into peals of laughter. "Tell her," someone said.

Cyndy gave a shrug. "You're the next one to have a baby."

"Oh, no, I'm not." Amy dropped the plastic baby as if it were a hot coal.

There was more laughter. "Too late. The baby never lies. I got it at Karla's shower and look." Stephanie rubbed her baby bump.

Karla nodded. "Somehow the baby always ends up with the right person."

Amy turned bright red.

"Amy? Do you and Diego want to tell us something?"

"We're not even married yet!" *And never will be.*

"Leave her alone." Cyndy patted her on her knee and gave her a motherly glance.

Stephanie started opening her presents. A soft, snuggly blanket patterned like a black and white soccer ball was followed by the cutest little cleats that Amy had ever seen. There were various outfits that would make Stephanie's little girl the best dressed baby on the planet. Stephanie finally pulled back the wrapping on a scrapbook full of photographs all lovingly put together by her friend Emily.

"I thought maybe when the baby is grown-up, she might want to see what you and Brandon were like before she came along," Emily said shyly.

"This is lovely, Emily. Thank you."

The scrapbook made the rounds, and when it got to Amy she flipped through it just to be polite. Emily was a true crafter, though, and each page sported a different theme created with stickers and hand-drawn lettering. Amy didn't know most of the people in the photographs until she got to a page with Diego on it. She zeroed in on the photograph immediately. Diego, Stephanie, and her husband Brandon stood outside a stadium. Diego was in the middle of the group and his arms were wrapped around his friends. They all looked incredibly happy.

"He's very handsome, your man. Isn't he." Cyndy said softly.

"Yes. He is." But that wasn't what she was looking at. She was sure she had never seen this picture of the three of them before, yet it seemed very familiar. Diego and friends outside the Atoms' stadium. It niggled at her. Where had she seen this before? And then it hit her like a thousand soccer balls. She had seen it before, except Stephanie and Brandon had been photoshopped for two very gay men.

"Stephanie? Who took this picture? The one of Diego and you guys." The scrapbook was her first clue. If she could follow the trail of the picture from who took it and how it got to Emily, she might able to ferret out who was sending the pictures to Horowitz's office. "I'd love a copy," she added. She held the scrapbook up to show Stephanie the picture. "Look at that smile."

Stephanie nodded. "Oh, that one. Diego did. It was on a timer, I think. He was playing with his new camera."

"Really?"

"Yeah, it was after the Seattle game. Brandon had given Diego two assists, and after the game he and Diego were just goofing around. Diego had a new camera so we took a picture. He should have a copy if you really want one."

"Thanks. I'll ask him."

"I may have an extra one," Emily said, from the other side of the room. "I sent out an e-mail to the players, and they sent me their pictures of Stephanie and Brandon. I could print one up for you."

"Oh, that would be really great." Her mind spun in a million directions. The chatter started up around her again, but the fun and games were over for Amy.

The second she got back home, she went looking for Diego. She found him on a rare day off, in the kitchen downing another one of his green drinks.

"Want some?" He held out the glass to her. He wore tight running shorts and a cut-off top. He had just come from the gym. Amy made a mental note to tell Knight that Diego should dress more like a jock even in his own home.

"No thanks." She made a funny face. "I like my greens whole and sautéed in a lot of butter."

Diego pointed to the hallway and mouthed, "Tammy." Amy nodded and switched into #Amiego mode. They were in the middle of another command performance.

"You sure? It'll put hair on your chest," he joked.

"I don't think either of us would like that. You drink it."

"Your loss." He knocked the slushy green liquid back in one gulp. "How was the party?"

"Good. I got the baby."

"Excuse me?"

"I got the plastic baby in my cupcake. It means that I'm the next one in the group to get pregnant."

Diego's eyes widened. He took two quick steps back as if she'd announced she had the bubonic plague. Amy stifled a laugh. *He must really think I'm fishing for a baby.* She tipped her head subtly to the hall, but Diego was so wrapped up in his panic he didn't see.

"Not now, of course. When we're married." She gave him a pointed stare and another subtle head tilt to the hallway where she could have sworn she heard a slight rustle. "I thought you'd be happy. You told me you couldn't wait to have kids. Remember?" Tammy was too shrewd and unless Diego started playing along there was no way she would buy this.

"Yes." Understanding flooded his eyes. "But we never really talked about how many. I come from a family of four, as you know."

Amy laughed. "Slow down, slugger. There was only one baby in the cupcake."

Diego laughed with her. Amy rapped the granite countertop with her knuckles. That should be enough for Tammy to chew on for a while. She made a move to go when Diego called her back.

"One seems like a lonely number for a kid growing up." Diego's expression turned thoughtful. Amy wondered if suddenly they were having a real conversation. The appeal of not having to watch all her words and innuendos grabbed her; she jumped into her answer with both feet.

"I never knew anything different, but yeah, looking back, I guess it was lonely." She shrugged. "And now that my parents are gone, this is when I really wish I had a brother or sister around." Diego closed the gap between them and rubbed her shoulder. A shadow moved in the hallway, and Amy leaned into his comfort for greater effect.

"How many do you really want?" she asked.

"Two, maybe. You?"

"I don't know. Two sounds good. A boy and a girl."

"I think, maybe," he said, dropping his voice, "I'd be a good dad."

"Oh, Diego, you'll be a great father." And she meant it, too. He would dote on his kids. Suddenly, she saw herself in Horowitz's shiny glass office signing a new addendum to the contract. Her throat constricted a little.

"But not right now. I need to figure out what I'm doing with my life first." If they were really having this conversation in this real/fake way she might as well lay it all on the line.

"And what is that?"

"Well, I've actually been thinking about that homework, soccer club thing we talked about. Are you still up for that?"

"I am. Paul said he would run a feasibility study on it," Diego said.

Amy knew she shouldn't hold her breath. There was no way that Knight was going to invest in her, someone who wasn't in this for the long haul. But it was a nice thought.

"With the right result the club could be up and running within six months," Diego said.

"Wow. That's great news." Amy was surprised how fast things could move when Diego really wanted them. She wanted to ask more questions, maybe even ask him to put pressure on Knight to deliver, but Diego's attention had drifted back to their earlier conversation. It had really captivated him.

"We would have beautiful kids, though." He'd gone all fanciful on her again.

"Yeah, we would. But they better have your left foot. Mine's a dud." Amy tried a humor injection to steer him back on track.

"Okay, and have your pull-back vee. You got great timing on that move. I saw it when we were at the park."

"I practiced that move every day after school for a year straight until I got it. It's all about the speed."

"You know most couples would talk about who has the best nose or eyes to pass on."

"Well, we're not most couples."

Diego ignored the double meaning. "You're telling me that that our kids can be ugly as sin itself if they got game."

"Yep. That's what I'm telling you. Although your smile wouldn't hurt."

Diego took the cue and turned on his smile.

"Yeah. That one, for sure," Amy said.

They settled against the counter comfortably. Were they actually becoming friends, or were they just playing this game a little too well now?

"Let's go upstairs. I want to give you a proper good night before I leave for Boston tomorrow." He darted a look to the hallway and grabbed her hand.

Amy put her best dreamy face on and reached up to give Diego a kiss on the cheek. If Tammy was watching this, the picture of a loving couple running upstairs would cast out all doubts she had about separate breakfasts. Someone scuttled away from the hallway before they entered.

Halfway up Amy pulled her hand free. "Oh, I forgot my purse. You go. I'll catch up."

She skipped down the stairs and darted back into the kitchen. The room was darker now as dusk was falling, but she could see her purse hanging from the back of the chair. She reached for it, and her hand stilled. Her skin prickled. She wasn't alone.

A figure leaned on the island with her head cradled in her hands. It was Casey. Could it be that Tammy hadn't been lurking in the hall, at all? Had it been Casey the whole time?

Casey looked up slowly and met Amy's gaze. Her eyes were the palest blue Amy had ever seen. Hurt, confusion, or maybe a mixture of both poured from them. Amy's heart dropped with a thud.

"You were the one in the hall?"

Casey nodded. A bright flush crept into her cheeks.

Amy closed her eyes. She hadn't meant to say it like that, as if she knew that Casey had been there all along. All of a sudden the conversation with Diego, which had seemed so clever when she thought Tammy was the eavesdropper, now seemed flat out mean. Casey was in love with Diego. Mia had practically announced it to the entire golf course on their grand day out. And now Amy had driven the stake farther into Casey's heart with all this baby nonsense. It took all Amy had not to pull Casey in her arms and smooth away the pain. Not that it would've worked. Casey wanted Diego, not her.

"I forgot my purse," she said. It was all she could manage.

"I wasn't...I mean, I didn't...I didn't mean to hear all that," Casey said.

"I'm so sorry. I didn't know you were there. If I did I would've—" Amy stopped mid-sentence. What would she have done? She was contracted into that conversation with pen and ink, which now felt like blood. The silence between them hung heavy in the air.

"I should've come out sooner, but I didn't want you to know that I overheard what you were saying." Casey shook her head, commenting on her own stupidity. "Look. I forgot to give Diego his gift cards for the trip. He likes to hand these out to some of the players since traveling with the team can be expensive. Can you give them to him?"

She held the thick envelope out for Amy to take. Their hands brushed lightly at the exchange. Amy's hand froze for just a second as she refused to pull the envelope from Casey's hand and lose the contact. If the room had been just a tiny bit darker, she could have imagined sparks actually jumping from one hand to the other, the charge ran quickly along Amy's arm. Slowly, she raised her gaze to meet Casey's hopelessly vulnerable stare.

"You're happy with Diego, right?" Casey finally broke the silence.

Amy nodded.

"I mean you're talking about having kids and all, I know. At least that is what I think I overheard." Casey paused. Her eyes turned steely. "I mean, I know I'm going way too far here, but is he the one?"

The knot of raw emotion tied up in Amy's heart ever since her parents' death unraveled slightly. A deep sadness seeped into her system.

She ached to fall headlong into those blue eyes and take this woman in her arms and tell her the truth. Inside she screamed, "No! No. He's not the one."

Casey raised her eyebrow. "Well, is he?"

Amy took a deep breath and held it in her lungs as she searched for the right thing to say. This was the moment. Come clean or stay dirty and get dirtier still? The truth weighed heavy on her tongue. Her contract sat locked away in Horowitz's office like a deal with the devil. The truth would destroy everything. And what would be the point of honesty now? It wasn't as if Diego and Casey were riding off into the sunset together.

"Yes," she said, softly. "He's the one." The loosened ends of the knot wrapped tight around her heart again.

Casey's eyes turned cold. She released the envelope and said almost breezily, "Good for you. See you tomorrow."

Her retreat was quick, leaving Amy alone in the kitchen. She stood there long enough for dusk to turn the marble counters inky black.

"I thought you'd gotten lost," Diego said when she finally returned to the apartment.

"In this house that's a real possibility," she said, marveling at how cheerful she sounded. "I couldn't find my purse. Turns out I left it in the car."

Her lies flowed like wine from a bottle. Amy wondered why she didn't come clean about Casey and her affection for Diego. He had, after all, asked her to check up on his P.A. and her happiness. But Amy was out of the habit of telling the truth, especially when the truth would humiliate Casey.

"What are you watching?" she asked.

Diego had turned on the TV and was now sprawled over her sofa completely at home.

"Sports Center," he said. "Do you mind? I thought it would be better if Tammy thought we were having a long goodbye. Did you see her down there?"

"No. Not Tammy."

On the TV an outfielder made a fantastic diving catch. "Ooh. Did you see that?" Diego said.

"I did." She stood up a little straighter and squared her shoulders. She had a job to do after all. "Hey, today at the party Emily gave Stephanie a really beautiful photo book of her and Brandon and all the players. There was one of you and them at the stadium."

"She did?"

"Yeah. How did Emily get it?"

"Get what?" Diego's stare was glued to the TV and the top ten plays of the day.

"The photo. Did she ask you?"

"What photo? Now that's a ball I would've liked to put in the back of the net."

The TV ran the goal in slow motion. A woman soccer player dressed in the white of Team USA threw her body up into the air. The ball rocketed into the back of the net with her scissor kick.

"The woman's game has really elevated. It's the play of the day," he said.

That woman could have been Casey if things had worked out differently. Amy rubbed her forehead.

"You have a headache?"

"No. No, I'm fine." She pushed her hand through her hair and tried again. "Stephanie said you took the picture with a timer on your camera. Right after the Seattle game? Brandon gave you an assist. No, I think it was two assists."

"Oh, that one. Yeah, I took it."

Amy imagined leaping over the couch and slamming the TV off. What was it about men and TV? She had seen it numb the brains of almost every man in the Valley Arms for years.

"But how did Emily get it?"

"Oh, that's a Casey question. You can ask her in the morning. She'll know."

Diego had shoved her right back in Casey's path. Karma was a bitch.

CHAPTER 8

"I E-MAILED EMILY THE PICTURE last month."
Casey sat behind her desk, impatience rolling off
her. "You couldn't text me these questions?" Her
unyielding gaze bored a hole into Amy's forehead.

Amy kept her feet planted on the floor, refusing
to move an inch. Diego had been chauffeured out
of town earlier that morning, so she was on her
own in this lion's den.

"Well, I could've, but I kinda wanted the SD
card if you had it."

"Why?"

The vulnerable woman from last night had
totally vanished. Instead someone made of steel
sat before her. Had their meeting in the kitchen
done that to her?

"It's a...present for Diego." She grimaced
slightly over the lie. Not one of her better ones.

"What is? The SD card?"

"No." Casey's relentless questions were
beginning to make her feel hunted. "I need the
pictures and any others if you have them. I want
to do a little collage for Diego." That was better.

"A collage?"

"Yeah. Of him and me and soccer. I'm crafty that way." Although at the moment she didn't feel at all crafty.

"Okay" Casey picked up a pen and began to tap it on a pad of paper. "I'll need to get Diego's permission first."

"Really?" Alarm bells rang in her head. "Why?"

"Because they're his pictures."

Amy tilted her head in thought. She was awfully protective of this SD card. Did Casey have any part in the photoshopped deliveries that showed up at Horowitz's office?

"But mostly because I work for him, not you," Casey continued.

There it was. She had nothing to do with the doctored photos; Casey was still pissed about last night. Amy didn't blame her. In fact, she had hesitated walking into the office this morning full of orders and rubbing salt in Casey's wounds from the night before. But now that Casey had thrown down the gauntlet Amy found she was ready for a fight.

"Okay. Text him," she said

"I will, and I'll let you know."

Amy plopped down on the leather sofa. "I can wait."

"You're kidding?" The annoyance in Casey's voice only made Amy settle in deeper.

"Nope." Amy crossed her legs and lifted a magazine. She had grabbed a soccer equipment catalogue. *Great, this will pass the time, yawner.*

With Casey's gaze still on her she studied the different sizes of work-out cones on page three as if they held the secret to the universe. A deep sigh came from the other side of the room followed by the sounds of Casey texting.

Amy formed a silent plea for a speedy reply. Diego had to be close to getting on the plane. She could be here for hours with this ridiculous stand, and the catalogue only had fifty pages.

Page thirty-five was a bonanza. Polyester mesh pull-over pinnies on one side, double-sided numbered vests on the other. Not about to lose this contest, she mentally began to compile a list of pros and cons. Amy finally heard the beep of Casey's phone.

Please, please, let it be Diego. She raised her gaze, twisting her face into a picture of indifference.

"Well?" she asked. "Is it Diego?"

"Yes."

"And?"

"He says that's fine."

"Perfect." Amy closed the catalogue. Casey, as if making a point, got up slowly, pulled a white binder from the bookshelf and slid an SD card from a protective pocket inside.

"Thanks." Amy held out her open palm.

"You're welcome." Casey dropped the SD card into her hand from two inches up. No fingers touching. No electric sparks. No whooshing in her chest. What a difference a day made.

"Anything else I can help you with?"

"No. Thank you for this." She squeezed the SD card tighter than she meant to.

"No problem." Casey turned her back on Amy. The realization that she had no way to view the card hit her as soon as she was halfway across the flagstones. She laughed at her own stupidity. There was no way she was turning around, so she walked straight into the kitchen where Tammy sat at the huge oak table sipping something frothy out of a coffee mug and doing a sudoku puzzle in the paper.

"Morning, Tammy." Amy effused all the cheer she could muster into her voice.

"Morning." Tammy hunkered down in her chair. She wasn't moving.

"I would like to look at this SD card. Where's Diego's computer?" She leveled a stare at the woman at the table.

"In his office." *Of course it was!* But Tammy's tone made her feel extra stupid.

Amy, who had already had her fill of challenging women that morning, waltzed out of the kitchen before Tammy could start up.

A brand new iMac and huge monitor greeted her as soon as Amy turned into the office. Amy dropped into the chair behind the desk and pushed the "on" button. The system sprang to life, only to immediately ask her for the password.

Amy rubbed her forehead. "What would Diego use?" she wondered out loud. A deep sigh followed. "His mother? The Atoms? Soccer?"

Amy smiled and typed in Dulce's name. The password was refused. Amy tapped the desk with her finger for a moment and then typed in Dulce with the number 10, Diego's jersey number, after it.

An almost blank desktop opened on to the screen. Cracking the password had been laughably easy. The only part of this puzzle that was. She tried not to look at the files; she was a practiced liar, but not a snoop. From the empty screen, it seemed Diego almost never fired this baby up. She slid the SD card into the processor and the pictures on the card jumped up in iPhoto. She viewed Diego with his family at a party, a bunch of action shots from the Seattle game with his new camera, a few of Dulce. She scanned through every single picture and not one, with the exception of the threesome at the stadium, looked anything like the photos that she remembered from Knight's envelope. So how had the blackmailer acquired the photos? There were other SD cards in that notebook, but unless Casey was the blackmailer, nothing made any sense.

"Damn," Amy said under her breath. She had entered the office with such hope. She leaned back in the chair, staring out into space. Everything was such a mess. Her easy solution to the mystery of the photographs shifted out of place like Tammy's puzzle. Get one little number wrong and the whole block went off.

In fact, everything was a mess. The relationship she had no interest in was perfect, while the non-relationship she obsessed over was a raging disaster. Every time she opened her mouth a lie came out, and Simon, the one person she would have confessed all her problems to, was still not talking to her.

Knight, you're wrong. This isn't some lame ass fairy tale. This is a full-on horror story. Amy closed her eyes and rolled her head back into the headrest of the chair. Actually, if this really were a fairy tale, she would look up and the answer to all her problems would be in front of her. She just had to recognize it. That's the way magic worked.

She opened her eyes and saw a wide expanse of desktop that looked like it was hardly ever used. The leather desk pad had no notes or reminders, the rectangular pen holder was empty, and the flip calendar was four months out of date. Four photographs were grouped on the desk corner. They looked like they'd been placed for show and then forgotten. This was a fail.

She was rolling around the conversation she would have with Knight in her head when one of the photo collection caught her eye. In the center of the group was a lovely picture of Diego in a bright teal T-shirt, bending down to kiss Abuelita on her cheek. She looked so happy, and Diego's expression brimmed over with love for the old woman.

"Son of a bitch!" She grabbed the photo. The answer had been right in front of her the whole time. This was another of Knight's photoshopped forgeries.

"Yes!" She pumped her fist and ran up the stairs to her apartment for her phone.

You're not going to believe this. I found some of the pictures! She texted Knight and added three of those grinning happy faces for good measure.

Her cell phone rang immediately. "Don't put it in writing." Knight's voice rumbled out from the phone.

"Sorry, I didn't realize this was black ops. Are we in blackout mode?"

"Amy, this isn't a joking matter. We need to be super careful. Everyone's livelihood depends on solving this. Diego's, yours, and mine, to mention a few."

"Yes, I know."

"What did you find out?"

"Well..." She drew out the word. She really liked, for once, having the upper hand with Knight. "I found the source of two of the pictures."

"Really?" His voice was incredulous.

"Yes, really. Do you want to hear the info now? Or do you want me to tell you in your soundproof room?"

"Funny. Just tell me now."

When she was finished silence greeted her.

"Then it's definitely someone with access to the house."

"Yeah, that's what I thought. But who?" she said.

"That's the million-dollar question. Tammy, Tom, even Casey, their jobs depend on Diego. If his well runs dry, so does theirs. You haven't noticed anything about them that we don't already know, have you?"

"No," Amy said quickly. She wasn't about to cheapen Casey's feelings for Diego by announcing them to Knight.

"Well, keep your eyes open," Knight said, and sighed audibly. "You're our only hope at the moment for getting to the bottom of this."

"That's your best pep talk?"

"Amy, look—"

"Never mind. I'm on it, for better or worse."

For the first time since she walked through the front door of Diego's house, Amy had true purpose in her step. Before she had passively slunk from room to room hoping not to run into Diego or Tammy. Now she marched through the house on a bizarre treasure hunt studying every picture she could find. The first one she uncovered hung on the wall right outside the gym. Diego held Dulce as a brand-new puppy Amy remembered a second handsome man in the doctored up version at the coffeehouse. She took out her cellphone to record her find. A little more searching and she found another sitting on the wet bar in the living room, Diego was getting out of the pool in the backyard during a family BBQ.

Dripping wet, he wore a skimpy Speedo revealing his gorgeous muscular body.

Amy pulled the photo off the bar for a closer look. This one almost didn't need any doctoring to make its point, but Amy remembered the false version had a bunch of men around him, not his nieces and nephews. The mantel in the den was a bonanza. Three different photographs from the envelope; the beach, the boat, and the garden, all right there in open view.

She raised her phone and took pictures of their positions on the mantel. She needed proof, but to move any of them would alert whoever was behind this.

"What are you doing?" Amy flinched. Tammy's harsh voice hit her from behind. Damn. How long had she been there standing at the kitchen door watching? Amy had been so focused she hadn't bothered to watch her own back. Rookie mistake.

She turned around trying to compose her expression. What had Tammy seen—but, more importantly, what did Tammy know? A picture of Diego in a compromising position hitting the internet would make it awfully hard for Amy to keep on living here. Surely that couldn't be the motive, could it?

Thinking fast she grabbed the picture of her and Diego at the park that was sitting right up front.

"I'm looking at me and Diego," she said, trying to infuse her words with a lightness that she really didn't feel. She quickly brought the picture over to Tammy moving away from more incriminating photos and giving her time to slide her phone into her pocket. "Aren't we a beautiful couple?"

"Yes. I guess so." Tammy took the picture from Amy's outstretched hand and brushed tender fingers over Diego's cheek. "Diego looks very handsome here."

"He always does."

Tammy met her gaze for a long moment. A warning that Amy couldn't read flashed in her eyes. "I'll put it back where it belongs."

"Thanks. We need more of me and Diego up there, don't you think?"

Tammy only grunted and dropped the picture in the back behind one of Diego and his mother.

Amy walked into the local library, the place where she had always done her best thinking. She felt upbeat. Her eyes shone with determination; she had this mystery by the tail. She took a padded chair at the back and scrolled through the photo evidence on her phone. She'd located half a dozen in just an hour of searching. The others had to be there, too. It led to only one conclusion: the offender absolutely had to be someone with access to the house. But who? Someone in his family who was jealous, perhaps? His family dropped by all the time. There was plenty of opportunity. Or maybe it was someone who already lived there?

Tammy? She had hated Amy from the moment she moved in, spying on her, throwing out snide little digs whenever she could. She'd been startled when she'd caught Amy by the photographs on the mantel. It could easily be her. She had access galore. Could Tammy have been preparing the ground with the first pictures? Had she become worried when Amy arrived and moved up her blackmail plans with the heavy duty porno pictures?

No. It was a stupid theory. It made no sense. Knight had hit the nail on the head when he'd said Tammy owed her livelihood to Diego. Why would she sabotage it? What's more, the first picture had arrived in Horowitz's office long before Amy had. All the great progress of the morning only brought her to a dead end. Amy groaned loud enough for an old man at the next table to her to shush her.

"Sorry."

"Young lady," he said, "if you'll take my advice, try reading a book and not your phone. The reason why all you young kids are so stuck these days is that you can't keep your eyes off these digital contraptions."

"You're right," Amy said. "What're you reading?"

"A classic." He turned the cover of the book in his hands towards her. A black steamboat sailed along a river through a dense jungle. "Joseph Conrad, *Heart of Darkness,* ever hear of it?"

She knew the cover all too well. She had traced her finger repeatedly along that same river as she wrote her master's thesis in a different library, in a different life.

"No," she lied, refusing to dwell on her unfinished masters.

"All you need to know is in books like these," he said.

"Thanks, but that life didn't really work out for me." Then she shivered, as she remembered the destructive lie at the central core of *Heart of Darkness.* Shit. Maybe, the old man did know it all.

The clash of metal against metal woke her up with a start.

Diego's back? A glance at her clock told her that he would be in pre-game warm-ups right about now on the East Coast. So who was downstairs? She dropped her head back into the pillow only to realize that whoever it was had access to the house.

She flung back the bedclothes, startling Dulce, who was curled around her feet. Pulling her hair hastily into a ponytail and not bothering to change out of her skimpy camisole and silk shorts, she dashed downstairs and peered through the frosted glass door of the gym.

Rob, Diego's trainer, sat at the leg press machine, sliding two huge weights up and down the rack. He let the last one go and the weights crashed to the bottom of the rack. Amy slid back into the hallway so he couldn't see her.

Her mind was spinning. Rob works out here? When Diego is gone? She had seen how he had looked at Diego. Was that motive enough to blackmail the man? He certainly had opportunity, but did he have access to the rest of the house?

The questions crashed around in her mind. The door opened and Rob strode out. She headed toward the stairway to her apartment. If he caught her, she could say she was just going upstairs. The footsteps, however, faded in the opposite direction. This was her opportunity to play Nancy Drew. She darted inside the gym to see if he had left anything incriminating.

Apart from his gym bag the room was empty, although it held the sour odor of sweat. There was nothing, and then she heard his footsteps coming back. She could stay put, dream up yet another lie and maybe give the game away. Or... she spun on her heel, looking for a way out.

At the far end of the room was another door. She had no idea where it led to, but she raced toward it anyway. She opened it and ducked into a closet just as Rob stepped through the door at the other end. She was in total darkness. Hands grabbed her, pulling her farther back into the tiny room. She stumbled over something that felt like a vacuum cleaner and fell backwards into a warm body. A woman's body. Breasts pushed against her back as she was caught and set upright

"Shush." A hand clamped over her mouth. "Be quiet," someone whispered in her ear.

Amy nodded, and the hand fell away to rest lightly on her hip. Her eyes adjusted to the dim light that seeped under the door, not that it helped her know who was behind her. She drew on her other senses for that. The height, the lean muscles, even the citrus shampoo smell gave away her captor's identity. Or maybe it was the hand resting on her hip exactly as it had done at Footgolf. This was Casey.

What was she doing here? Hiding? Or something much worse? Amy's stomach knotted. She hated looking at everyone in the household with new suspicion. But anyone of them could be the culprit. She would have to wait for her answers until Rob cleared out. All they could do now was hold out in this tiny closet, which was not big enough for two.

Despite knowing better, she let her body sink back, just a little. Casey's breasts pressed fully into her back and warm breath danced delicately across the nape of her neck. Casey's shampoo smelled light and fruity with something much more spicy and organic underneath. Amy slowly registered first one place where they touched, and then another. Casey's fingers resting gently on her hip, her thigh braced against Amy's, her cheek against Amy's hair. It was delicious. Amy drank it all in and hoped that Rob's session lasted for another two hours.

Sadly, a bag zippering shut announced Rob's imminent departure. Amy registered the noises as he made his way out of the gym.

"He's gone," Casey whispered, and pushed Amy gently away. "Time to go."

Time for answers. Instead of walking out, Amy spun around in the closet creating a little space between them and bumped the door open with her hip, just enough to see Casey's face clearly. It was tantalizingly close. So close she could feel the warm breath on her cheek. She could see her lips trembling, and then she found Casey's eyes. Amy took a sharp intake of breath. Casey's eyes were dark and smoldering. The chill had completely melted away leaving a heat that could lure a girl into a thousand unthinkable things.

Suddenly, Casey's lips were on hers. Or was it the other way around? She couldn't think. Their lips came together in a hard and passionate kiss. Casey's mouth moved exquisitely over hers, taking full possession. Amy staggered, legs trembling, as the force of the kiss took her by surprise. No fantasy had prepared her for this. She had to take a step away from Casey to steady herself.

Casey looked at her questioningly but didn't say a word, her jaw clenched as if she were holding herself back. And then, losing the battle, her arms reached out for Amy's hips and dragged her back into the embrace. Heat rushed through Amy. Teeth nipped gently at her lips, and Casey's caressing tongue soothed the tingling. Desire exploded in Amy's chest.

And then nothing.

Only overwhelming emptiness as Casey broke away and ran from the storage room.

Amy was stunned. Her lips were bruised, and her whole body still shivered from the embrace. She could feel the pressure of Casey's mouth. The real thing blew her fantasies out of the water.

She knew what she should do. She had to let this moment go. She should chase after Rob and find some way to salvage her mission. She should step back, mentally and physically, from a very awkward situation with Casey. Instead, she rushed to the kitchen.

"Have you see Casey?" she asked Tammy.

"Yes. She just ran out the back. What's going on?"

"Nothing." Amy quickly slid past Tammy, heading directly for the pool office. One glance at Tammy's face told her that the woman wasn't buying "nothing" as an answer. Shit. Amy added Tammy to the list of people and things that she would have to deal with later.

She raced to the office and froze. Casey was simultaneously pulling papers from her desk drawer, grabbing her computer, and shoving everything into a large messenger bag sitting on the chair behind her.

"What are you doing? Leaving?" Amy stepped into the office.

Casey looked up and blushed from the roots of her hair all the way down her throat.

"Yeah. I'll text Diego and tell him."

"As in quitting?" Amy couldn't believe it.

Casey dropped her gaze, and if it were possible turned a deeper shade of red. "I am so sorry."

"I know. I shouldn't have—" *Wait. Is she apologizing?* Confusion played over Amy's face. "Sorry for what?"

A moment of silence hung between them. Something close to annoyance flitted through Casey's eyes, but was quickly replaced by a look of repentance. "For what happened in the gym. I don't know what came over me. You were just so close...And I had been..."

Amy said nothing as the shock of what Casey was implying washed over her. *I can't be this dense, Can I? Did Casey want that as much as I did?*

"Look," Casey continued, "I know you and Diego are practically married." She shoved a small purple notebook into the messenger bag and slid the drawer shut with a decisive click. "For Christ's sake, you told me he was the one the other night." She slung the bag over her shoulder and took two steps into the middle of the room facing Amy. "But back there, in the gym, when I was spying on Rob. You were so close. And, out by the pool the other day, I thought you were sending me signals...or trying to tell me something." Casey noticed the shock on Amy's face and groaned in misery. "Forget it. I don't know what I thought..."

Yes! Casey had been thinking about her too. Amy stared, unable to turn her excitement into coherent words.

"Whatever. It doesn't matter now. I'll text Diego and tell him." Casey hoisted the bag higher up on her shoulder and headed to the door.

"I was." Amy cringed, though not from the words. The first truth she had told in weeks sent her heart soaring. And this particular truth could also bankrupt her or even send her to jail.

Casey froze, her hand about to grab the door handle. "You were what?"

"Trying to tell you something."

Casey slowly turned to face her. She stood with her back against the door and met Amy's gaze head on. "What? What were you trying to tell me?"

The moment of truth. If she opened her mouth and went down this path, there was no going back. The memory of the kiss played against her lips and brought a new kind of freshness to her heart. She would do anything to get back into Casey's arms. The price was high though. The image of Knight looming over her like an evil troll popped into the head. However, the price of lying to Casey was higher than breaking Horowitz and Kane's non-disclosure contract. She needed to move forward in her life, and playing the big boys' game was not healthy for her. She needed to trade her fake relationship for a real one.

"Well? What were you trying to tell me?" Casey said again. Amy guessed that neither of them wanted to make the first move. Neither of them wanted to be wrong about this.

"That I..." What the hell, just go for it. "That from the moment you crawled out of the pool that first day...I've just wanted to do this." She stepped up and grabbed Casey by the waist pulling her forward. Her mouth was already tipped upward for the kiss. It was softer, more tentative than the one in the gym. As soon as their lips met, Amy felt Casey shiver in her arms, and she went dizzy with the realization she'd been the one to cause it. The kiss deepened, and Casey once again broke away. This time she took Amy's hand and dragged her across the office into the small bathroom.

"Tammy might see." Her explanation was brief before she dropped her lips back onto Amy's.

The bag dropped from Casey's shoulder onto the floor. Neither worried about the computer inside. Amy wrapped her arms around Casey's strong body and pulled her close as Casey wound her fingers into Amy's long hair. Their bodies crushed against each other, and Amy fell into the kiss completely. She moaned as Casey's tongue sought the sweetness of her mouth with the gentlest of touches, teasing her, making her want more. Darla had never kissed her like this. Amy didn't know kisses like this existed. Whatever the cost would be, it was totally worth it.

Casey grabbed her and lifted her up so she sat on the edge of the sink, her thighs wrapped around Casey's hips. A rush of heated expectation caught at her chest making her breathing ragged. Goosebumps spread across her skin. She felt her nipples harden until they were almost painful.

I need to slow this down. She gasped for air as Casey's lips sucked on an earlobe, her hands firmly kneading Amy's backside.

"Are we only going to do this in tiny rooms where there's barely enough space to stand up?" she muttered into Casey's throat, gently nipping the tanned flesh.

"No. I hope to do this lying down at some point." Casey's hands slid under her camisole and up her spine.

Amy blushed hotly. A little moan escaped her.

"Too soon?" Casey asked. A secretive smile played around her lips.

"No. Yes. Maybe a little."

"I don't want this to be a one-time thing." Casey nibbled her neck.

"Me neither. But it's complicated in so many ways," Amy mumbled, savoring the touch. She was losing control. "Besides, I thought you liked Diego."

"Of course I like Diego." Casey trailed kisses across her collar bone, slipping the lacy strap off her shoulder.

"I mean in that way. I mean, this way. You know like, like..." Amy was having a hard time concentrating.

Casey pulled back to look her in the eyes. "Where did you get an idea like that?"

Amy thought back. "Tammy, I guess."

Casey snorted. "Figures. No. I've liked girls since the moment I got my first Barbie doll and wanted to do this to her." She slid her hand down Amy's bare shoulder "It's Tammy who has the hots for Diego. Just look at the way she stares at him all the time. If she could, she would eat him up." Casey's caress froze and her expression turned thoughtful. "Diego knows about you, right?"

Amy's heart somersaulted in her chest. "No. It's complicated," she said again.

Casey took a real step back as far as the tiny room would let her.

Amy felt the warmth leave her side as if someone had turned off the sun.

"How complicated?" Casey asked simply, but suddenly there was a hard edge to her tone. "I'm not going to do this if Diego gets hurt."

What if it's just me who gets hurt? "Neither would I." She reached out to pull Casey to her again.

"Exactly what is going on between you and Diego?" Casey resisted her tugging and shifted her weight uneasily from foot to foot.

Of course, Casey wasn't going to let her get away with anything. Amy liked her way better for it, but it made getting out of this moment harder than ever. A dozen lies sprang up like bitter weeds on Amy's tongue. Any one of them might put Casey at ease and get her back into Amy's arms. A shiver, and not the good kind, ran over her body. She was getting too good at lying. She pursed her lips. Time to come clean. Time to really move forward—no matter what the price.

"Let's go out and get a cup of coffee, and I'll tell you the whole story," she said.

"Okay." Casey's gaze dropped down to her body. "But you might want to change first."

Amy looked down. Son of a gun. She was still in her pajamas.

CHAPTER 9

AMY ZIPPED THROUGH THE GATES of Hidden Hills
down past Caffeine Cowabunga's parking lot,
and straight on into her old neighborhood. She
pulled up before a coffee shop attached to a
dilapidated bowling alley. She figured the truth
would come easier if she were in surroundings
that were more her own.

There was no one at all in the greasy spoon
midmorning and in the middle of the week.

"I love places like this," Casey said. It was
the first time she'd spoken since they'd left the
office. Her approval eased the tension closing in
on them since their bathroom kiss.

"Anywhere you want." The waitress waving
her hand at the empty diner.

Amy chose a booth in the back, and they
ordered two coffees.

"Okay, so spill. What's going on?" Casey got
right down to business

Amy sighed. "I know so little about you. Just
three things maybe. One, you're great at Footgolf;
two, a super cool ten-year-old thinks you hang

the moon; and three, you're a really, really good kisser."

Casey blushed. Their coffees arrived, and they waited until the waitress left before continuing.

"Well, you are," Amy said. "And I would like to kiss you again—very much." She tamped down the desire that quickly rose in her. "But there are so many reasons I shouldn't tell you this story. Especially the parts that aren't mine to tell. And only one good reason why I should."

"What's that?"

Amy glanced down at her bare left hand. She stretched the fingers. Her whole hand felt lighter without the big fake rock on her ring finger. It sat on her dresser at home. This conversation would be easier without it.

"You," she said. "You're the reason. I pray you're worth it, and I'm not another idiot making big decisions using the wrong part of my body."

"Okay." Casey drew out the word, she looked a little offended.

"Shit. See, I haven't even started and I've already screwed up. Just hear me out. Will you?"

"That's why I'm here."

Once she got started the story rolled out more easily than she thought it would. Casey settled in on her side of the booth. Amy stumbled over the part about Diego's being gay. But Casey leaned forward and cupped Amy's hand on the table to give her strength.

"I always thought he was," she said softly. "I think anyone who looks carefully can see it. Except maybe Tammy." She chuckled, and again the tension dissipated.

Amy finally finished. She waited for Casey's response. "And how much does Knight pay you to do this?"

"A lot. Enough to make me feel a little bit dirty about it."

Casey raised her eyebrow in a question.

"Fifteen hundred a week," Amy said.

"Damn. I got the wrong job." An amused smile played at Casey's lips. "How would Knight feel about polygamy? That would send Diego's machismo through the roof, don't you think."

Amy laughed.

"Does Knight know that you're gay?"

"No. He doesn't." Amy paused rolling the next thought around in her head. "I'm going to be truthful with you. The way your kisses made me feel back there made me know for sure I one hundred percent like women. I like you, but I haven't had a whole lot of experience. I had a sort of girlfriend in college. Her name was Darla; she was a law student. But that didn't go as far as it could have." She looked over at Casey. Did she really want to take all of this on?

"That we can remedy."

Amy blushed.

"Well, we can. That's the easiest and most fun part of this puzzle to solve." Casey's eyes flashed. "So what were you doing in the gym?"

Amy had left the Photoshop situation out of her confession. Why, she wasn't sure. She thought, at least she hoped, that Casey had nothing to do with the envelopes that showed up at Horowitz's office. "Why where you there?" she asked back.

"I asked you first," Casey said, playfully.

"Yeah, but it's your turn to answer the hard questions. Why were you spying on Rob?" Amy rubbed her hand across her forehead.

"Trust has to go both ways. Is that what you're saying?"

Amy nodded.

"Okay. It's going to sound weird, though."

"Really?" Amy laughed. "Weirder than what I just told you?"

"You be the judge." Casey spun her spoon on the table top while her eyes darted back and forth in thought. "Rob has always given me the heebie-jeebies. You know he's not a real trainer. I mean, he's not certified or anything. And I don't like the fact that Diego lets him work out in the gym when he isn't around. About a month ago I caught him in the house, and not the kitchen where he enters and exits. When I asked him about it, he said he was just taking a look around. I know that Diego would let him do that, but the vibe was weird. So I've kind of been keeping an eye on him." She leaned forward and raised her eyebrows. "Today when I got to work, I saw him in the den, hovering around the mantel. He took, at least I think he did, a photo and put it under his shirt."

"Really?" The pieces started to come together. "So you followed him?

"Of course. Wouldn't you? I mean, he shouldn't be roaming around the house in the first place, and certainly not taking things. I wanted to find out what he was doing with it."

"Did you?"

"No, I got into the gym before he did and hid in the back to see what he was up to. But when he came in he just dumped his bag on a bench and worked out. I don't even know if he actually took the picture or not. He could've been just scratching his chest or something. I was waiting for a clean exit when you came in and changed everything."

"I'm glad I did." Amy grinned at her.

"Me, too." Casey smiled right back. "So basically I got nothing. Your turn."

Casey's eyes opened wider and wider with each new detail as Amy told her about the envelopes arriving at Horowitz's office, the photoshopped pictures inside, and the fact that the originals all had come from Diego's home.

"Wow, that's better than the first story you told me." Casey dug around in her messenger bag and pulled out her wallet.

"What're you doing?"

"Paying. We gotta get back to the house to see if he took a picture and if he did, which one he took."

Casey flipped open her wallet and dropped some bills on a table. Amy sat back, watching. Her movements were efficient and fluid and possessed a grace that made her a pleasure to watch, and probably deadly on the soccer field. Amy idly began to imagine that grace in other areas as well, like bed. Heat stole into her cheeks.

"Here, let me contribute." Amy pulled her own wallet out of her back pocket.

"No." Casey placed her hand on Amy's arm which immediately started tingling under her touch. "You get the next one."

The heat quickly spread across her whole face. There was going to be a next one.

Casey and Amy stood in front of the mantel in the den, their shoulders almost touching. The house was empty, and Amy noticed how their personal space had changed thanks to the morning activities. A very happy change, at that.

"You see anything different?" Casey asked, bringing her back to the matter at hand. At a first glance, the pictures on the mantel looked like they always did.

"Hey, wait a second. Where is the one of me and Diego? The one with the mountains?"

"That was here?"

Amy tapped a space right in the middle of the wood beam. "It was right here."

"You sure?"

"Yeah. I saw it yesterday. Look." She took out her cell phone and showed Casey the picture as it sat on the mantel the day before. "Tammy put it back last night."

"I knew it. Rob must have taken it this morning."

"Why? Why would he do that? I mean don't you think it's odd that he's going to all this trouble to doctor the photographs?"

"It wouldn't be all that much trouble," Casey said thoughtfully. "He freelances as a graphic artist. That's his real job."

"You're just telling me this now?"

"I just thought of it." Casey shrugged.

"Okay. So he has the opportunity to take the photos, the ability to change them into whatever he wants, but what's the motive?" Amy bumped her shoulder into Casey's to give the question emphasis, but mostly she just wanted to feel Casey's warmth again.

"Clearly not money." Casey bumped her back and left her shoulder resting against hers. "Which is kinda weird, because I don't think he works full time."

"Could it be an attention kind of thing?" Amy blew out a long breath. "We're really no further along than when we were hiding out in the closet."

"So let's get some proof."

"How? We can't just go up to him and say, hey are you kind of, sort of blackmailing Diego?"

"No, but we can get him to talk in another way."

"How?"

"We're going to put some of that easy money you make to good use."

"Believe me it hasn't been that easy with you around to tempt me."

Casey rewarded her with a smile that melted her heart. "It went both ways. You just didn't know it."

Twenty minutes later, they stood in an electronics aisle at Best Buy, looking at all sorts of surveillance cameras.

"Look. You can put this one in a teddy bear. Oh, cool, it actually comes with the teddy bear." Amy tapped on one box near the end of the row.

Casey, who had already bypassed the nanny cam section, studied a bigger box a section down from Amy. "I think we need something more like this. It records as well as lets us see what's going on."

"That's huge." Amy joined her. "You don't think Rob will see it."

"Only this part," Casey pointed to a small white camera with a black eye, "sits in the room somewhere. We could easily hide it by the TV. With all the devices Diego has there, Rob won't notice at all. I mean it almost looks like the connect thingy from the Xbox."

"I guess so."

"This"—she pointed to something that looked like the bastard baby of a CPU and a DVR—"records everything. We could sit up in your apartment and watch. Or come in later and review the tape."

"Wow. Okay let's get it."

"It's a lot of money. And I'm not really in a position to help you." Casey pursed her lips and glanced back down at the price tag. Amy followed her gaze and nearly choked at the total of the big black numbers. Good causes didn't come cheap.

"Don't worry. I'll save the receipt and submit it to Knight as a work expense."

Casey loosened up. "Okay. Serves him right. Let's get it."

When they pulled into the driveway, Tammy's car was still absent.

"Where do you think she is?" Amy asked.

"I don't know. She's never around when Diego's out of town. Let's not look a gift horse in the mouth."

They carried the box between them into the house and straight up into Amy's apartment. Casey did all the heavy lifting as Amy directed her to the coffee table.

"Whew." Casey shook out her fingers and started to unpack all the components. Amy opened the fridge and said a little thank you that she had gone shopping the day before. The shelves were full of fresh vegetables and gourmet cheeses, all the treats that she neither had the time or money to try before Diego.

"You hungry?" she asked, breaking the silence in the room.

"I am, actually."

"I can make sandwiches."

"Sounds great."

Amy grabbed a sharp cheddar cheese, tomatoes, bypassed the red onions, and held her hand over the two packets of meat.

"Ham or chicken?"

"Ham."

Amy pursed her lips; she would have put money on the chicken.

"Cheese?" Now she was completely in the dark.

"Please."

"Mayo, mustard, or butter."

"Mustard. Who puts butter on a sandwich?"

"They do in England. Cheese, tomato, and butter. It's actually good. I'll give you a bite of mine."

Amy let all the ingredients tumble onto the counter. Now she could watch Casey assemble the surveillance cameras as she put together the sandwiches. Amy marveled that they had so easily fallen into set roles.

Casey sat on the couch taking up the space around her like she owned it. She methodically unpacked the whole box and organized the components on the coffee table to mirror the picture in the instructions that were spread open on her lap. They worked in comfortable silence until Amy joined her, handing over the ham sandwich on a paper plate. The bread was lightly toasted, and Casey bit into it with a satisfying crunch.

"Oh my God. This is really good." She cleared a place on the coffee table for them both.

"I like to cook," Amy said shyly. "When I have a reason to."

"Count me reason number one." Casey took another large bite. She tweaked the camera set-up and connected it to her iPhone showing Amy the picture as it recorded.

"I think we're ready. Now we just need to go downstairs and set the camera up in the den."

Easier said than done. Tammy had returned and was doing something loud and noisy in the kitchen. They huddled in the hallway their faces almost touching.

"We can't both go in there," Casey whispered. "I'm hardly ever in the house when I work here. I stay in my office as much as I can. Tammy sees me as competition for Diego's attention."

"Yeah—me too."

Casey stifled a laugh. "If she only knew." Her hand brushed against Amy's forearm. Amy pressed into the touch. It had only been a couple of hours since their bathroom kiss and

Amy already missed the contact. She reluctantly pulled away.

"You go to the office. I'll set it up. I've already told Tammy a stupid lie about making a photo collage for Diego." She took the small recording device from Casey. "You can see the whole room through your phone, right?"

"I can. And I can also text you if we need to change something."

"Sounds like a plan."

Amy watched Casey sneak out a side door. Only when she was completely across the flagstones, did Amy move into the den. Even though she had never touched an Xbox, she had watched Simon play all the time when they lived together. She placed the recorder camera in the TV cabinet among the rest of Diego's boy toys. A clatter of pots and pans from the kitchen caused her to work quickly. She stepped back, looked into the camera and gave it a thumbs up mouthing an okay to Casey

Her phone beeped almost immediately with a text. *A little to the left.*

Amy made the adjustment and waited. *Perfect.*

She blew a kiss into the camera and wandered into the kitchen just to make sure that Tammy didn't suspect anything. Tammy was measuring out careful amounts of flour and sugar into the mixing bowl. She turned when Amy entered and for once was not wearing her habitual scowl.

"The game's over," she said, happily. "Diego scored the only goal. The Atoms are at the top of their division."

"Isn't that great?" Amy said, a little ashamed that she had completely lost track of the kickoff time. "So you're baking him a cake?"

"A sugar-free carrot cake. His favorite."

"He'll love it." Amy turned to go and her phone pinged with a new text. *What are you doing?*

Her thumbs moved over the screen. *Taming the beast.* "That's Diego." Amy looked up from her phone lying easily. "He's says hi."

"He does?" Tammy looked at Amy wistfully.

"Yes, he's asks about you all the time. I should've told you. He'd be lost without you, you know."

It was that easy. Tammy melted into a pool of devotion. Her face suddenly looked ten years younger as she gave Amy her first genuine smile.

"Oh, I almost forgot. These came for you earlier." She picked up two tickets on the counter and handed them to Amy. "Who are the Plastic Zippers?"

"My friend's band. They're playing tomorrow. Diego and I are going."

"Don't keep him out too late; he's in training, you know."

"Yes, Tammy."

Amy sat on her couch reading. She and Casey had a rendezvous and she kept glancing over at the soccer ball clock on the wall for what seemed like the umpteenth time. Only three minutes had passed since she had last looked. Casey had texted at four o'clock to say that she would ditch her car, then get a ride back to the house. That was three hours ago. Where is she ditching her car? Two cities over? There had been enough time for Amy to take a shower, fluff her hair at least a dozen times, and read almost all of a thin paperback.

Finally, there came a noise at the door. Amy leaped up sending the book flying. When she opened the door Dulce pranced inside and headed straight for the sofa. She pawed the cushions and then plopped down with a happy groan.

"An adorable girl, but not the one I was waiting for." Amy went to swing the door shut only to see Casey standing further down the hall, trying to suppress a smile. She held a pizza box and a six-pack of beer.

"You think I'm adorable?"

"You've got to stop eavesdropping in hallways." She tried to sound severe, but her goofy smile gave her away.

"But this is something I actually want to hear."

Amy pulled her into the room and shut the door. "Did Tammy see you?"

"No. I waited until she and Tom disappeared to their apartment."

"Is that what took you so long?" Amy asked.

"Well, I didn't want to come back empty-handed, but mostly I had to wait for my brother to get off work to drive me back over here." She moved to the kitchenette. Amy realized that she had taken some time with her appearance. Gone were the black T-shirt and the soccer shorts. Instead, she was wearing a cute button-up tank top that showed off the muscles in her arms. Her cotton shorts were high-cut, highlighting legs that went on forever.

"We're going to have to heat this up." She offered up the pizza box.

Amy was quick to get it into the oven and then onto plates. They chatted easily while they ate.

"I love artichoke hearts." Amy crunched on the last slice. "Where did you get this?" Dulce sat at their feet, hoping for crumbs.

"In Tarzana. There's this place—"

"No wait. Don't tell me. It's better for my waistline not to know."

Casey laughed and threw up her hands. "Okay. But if you change your mind. I'll take you there."

"Like on a date?"

"Yes. If you want to."

"I do."

After they cleaned up, Casey turned on her cell phone, and they crowded over the phone to look at a full frame of the den. The recorder had a fish-eye lens which elongated the whole room from the mantel all the way to the bar on the other side.

"This is really good," Casey said, as she pointed to both doorways. "We can track him from the moment he walks in to the moment he walks out and everything in between."

Their heads touched as they both crammed in to stare at the tiny screen. "I had a lot of fun today," Amy said, softly.

"I did too." Casey laughed from deep in her throat. Amy shivered. She had never heard a laugh so sexy. "And that's something. Because I was still so mad at you and that stupid stunt you pulled yesterday with the SD card." Casey bonked her playfully with her hip. "Hey, how long would you have sat rooted on that sofa, anyway?"

"As long as it took. But I was scraping the bottom of my patience with that soccer catalogue."

"Well, it worked. I was furious."

"How did you think I felt when you told me that you only worked for Diego?"

Casey laughed. "The joke's on me. Little did I know that you worked for him, too. But I'm glad to know that I got to you."

"Then and now." Amy bit her bottom lip nervously.

Casey responded at once. She touched Amy's forehead with her own. "Good. I'm glad I get to you."

Amy froze, unsure how to navigate what came next. Casey, full of ideas, nuzzled her neck. Her gentle breath played against Amy's skin as she traced a line to her chin with soft little kisses. A sweet tingling filled Amy's belly, and she finally relaxed. *I could spend the rest of my life doing this.*

Casey nibbled delicately at her lips, coaxing them open. With the tip of her tongue, she teased Amy's lips open and slid inside. Their tongues met. *God, she tastes good.* Their kiss deepened. Casey's hand slid under her shirt and trailed upward until her fingers grazed the side of Amy's breast. Amy groaned as Casey's fingers fluttered.

And then something else fluttered. On her thigh. No, it was more of a vibration.

"Your phone." Amy pulled back.

"What?"

"Your phone. It's vibrating."

Casey grabbed her phone to throw it off the couch. "It can't be anything important." But as she turned the screen towards her she froze. "Oh my God! It's working."

She flashed the phone at Amy. The downstairs den showed on the screen. Someone was moving over by the bar.

"Is that Rob?" Amy sat up straighter.

"No." Casey moved the camera into a close-up. "It's Tammy."

Tammy moved around the bar touching the pictures, rearranging them, until the one of

Diego coming out of the pool in his tight, tiny Speedo was front and center.

"What's she doing? You don't think she's in on this, too?"

Tammy ran her fingers lovingly over the photo of Diego, then raised it to her lips.

"Oh, man," Casey said. A look of horrified amusement covered her face. "She's into something else entirely."

"We shouldn't watch." Amy reached for the phone and turned it face down on the coffee table. There was something very sad about Tammy standing in a darkened room kissing the picture of the man she worked for.

"Maybe it's the kiss of a mother?" Casey shrugged, but her face didn't look very hopeful.

"Maybe." Amy pushed the phone further away. "Everyone deserves to have a few secrets, right." She reached out for Casey. She ached to be back in her embrace. Casey resisted.

"It might be time for me to go."

Amy's eyebrows arched in surprise. "Why?"

"I don't think...I'm not entirely sure this is a good idea."

"What?" Hurt and confusion flooded Amy. Hadn't she just risked everything breaking the contract with Knight by telling Casey the truth? And now she was backing off? "You don't like this? Like us?" There could only be one reason. Casey had taken a taste and that was enough.

Maybe it was all about conquest for her. She was an athlete after all.

Casey snorted. "No, that's the problem. I like it too much."

"How's that a problem?" Amy reached for her again. Casey intertwined their fingers, once again stalling the embrace.

"Amy. I think we should take this slowly. I mean I could stay. I want to stay, believe me I do. It's all I've been thinking about since I saw you in that dressing room in those skin tight Adidas." Amy blushed, and Casey raised her hand to her cheek. "But I want more than tonight, and I don't want to ruin that by moving too fast now."

Amy met her gaze. Her eyes were the blue of a mountain lake. She could look into those eyes forever, studying the changing moods of this woman. "So we won't move too fast tonight, and then you won't have to go," she said.

"You think it's that simple?"

"I do. Besides you don't have your car. I'd have to give you a ride home or you'd have to wait for your brother. In any case, you absolutely have to be here in the morning when Rob gets here. You need to work the camera." Amy held her breath. Had she just invited Casey to stay the night? "You can sleep on the couch," she quickly added.

"I don't want to rush you into anything you're not ready for."

"I think I'm ready for you to sleep on the couch."

Casey hesitated. Amy scooted away to give her space and grabbed the TV remote. "I should find the game. Diego likes to talk about it when he gets home." She pulled Dulce into her lap as a clear barrier between them.

Casey bit her lip and looked down at her hands. "Try BeIN Sports. The Mexican feed. They sometimes have replays of the games. I don't know what channel it is on Diego's network. Just scroll up the menu."

"Thanks." It was decided then. Taking things slow now translated into watching soccer with the woman she was infatuated with. Well, it could mean worse things.

"Want a beer?" Casey asked.

"Sure."

Casey brought in two beers from the kitchenette.

Meanwhile, Amy found the station and the game. Mexican Spanish came buzzing out of the TV's tiny speakers. It was the middle of the first half, the score zero-zero, and Diego was in fine form. He floated around the field receiving passes, setting up shots, and generally playing one step ahead of the men around him.

"He's looking good lately. You're good for him."

"It's not just me. He thinks the envelopes have stopped coming."

"Really? And whose idea was that?" Casey sounded surprised.

"Horowitz's or Knight's. I don't know which. Whoever was pulling the puppet strings that day."

"That seems like a big risk. Not to tell him the truth."

"You're telling me." Amy's voice rang with passion. "I think about how easy it is to get trapped in a lie all the time now."

"And sometimes they're even the lies you tell yourself." Casey ran a finger across the faded scar on her own knee.

"GOOOAAALLL!" The shout came from the TV.

"Damn. We missed it." Amy scooted Dulce off her lap. The TV flashed to a close-up of Diego, jumping up and down, in the middle of an Atoms' group hug. "Son of a biscuit. That's the only goal of the game. Tammy said so."

"They'll show it again." The TV, as if obeying Casey's command, cut to Diego. His shot blistered across the penalty box. The goalkeeper dived into its path, but the ball bounced out of reach and elegantly into the opposite corner of the goal.

"Wow." Casey sank back into the cushions and slid her hand up Amy's leg. "You know he makes it look so easy, but he had to thread a needle to get that in. Not that I have to tell you that. I've seen you on the field. Did you play in college?"

"Yeah, but not at a D-1 school and not for the national team."

Casey flinched and pulled her hand away from Amy's leg. "I never actually played for the national team," Casey said softly. "I never got the chance. Diego told you that part, right?"

"He said you would have taken the team by storm."

A thin smile played at Casey's lips. "That's sweet of him. But, honestly, we'll never know." She let out a breath. "I go back to that day a lot in my head." A slight bitterness crept into her voice.

"You don't have to talk about it if you don't want to."

"No. I actually think I do. That is if you want to hear about it."

"More than anything."

Casey shifted a few times in her seat before she finally started talking. "I should have blown the scrimmage off. It meant nothing to UCLA or me, but I was...it became...well let's just say that I played when I shouldn't have. I was heading for the goal on a breakaway and a sure hat trick. Just me and the goalie. She took me down one step out of the box. She got a red card, and I got a trip to the hospital. We didn't even get a penalty kick out of it." Casey's voice faltered. Amy took her hand and kissed the inside of her palm twice.

"Life doesn't go as we plan it," Amy said.

"The plan was to play soccer, get a free ride to UCLA, and apply to medical school. Then the plan was put med school on hold and play for the national team, and then the plan was rehabbing. And then there was no plan."

"Yeah. I know that last plan all too well."

"That's what people forget. Everyone has a story." She squeezed Amy's hand tightly. "What's yours? I've seen how you stare off into space sometimes. Not that I'm watching or anything."

"Ooh. Revealing our secrets? Are we there already?" Amy said lightly, but filed away the fact that Casey was very observant.

"Not if you don't want to go there yet."

Did she want to go there? She hadn't talked about any of it. To anyone. Ever. It seemed the day for taking leaps.

"My parents died when I was in college." She jumped right in with no preamble. "And I just kind of dropped out of school and life. The weird thing is that I don't really know why. There were money issues with school, but that wasn't really it. You know, the day I keep going back to is the day before they died, when I spoke to my mom on the phone. I actually called to tell her about Darla. I didn't know it then, but I think I was calling to come out to them. When I started, she just shut me down with some stupid remark about a gay movie they'd seen. It wasn't even a bad comment. It just put me off stroke, and I chickened out or thought I would do it later. I don't know." Casey squeezed her hand, and Amy remembered to breathe. "Then, suddenly, there was no later, and I felt like there was no me either. I'd lost the chance to grab who I was."

Casey placed the hand she was holding on her chest. "Now I'm sorry," she whispered. "That makes a bum knee sound like a walk in the park. My parents, my brother, my whole family were with me every step of the way. I wouldn't have gotten through it without them."

"No. It's okay. Like you said, everyone has a story." Amy's shoulders lifted. Telling hers out loud did wonders. Those thorny pieces in her heart softened. They would always be there, snagging at her when she least wanted them, but maybe, if she didn't hold back and had Casey with her, she could brush them aside. "I don't want to move slow, Casey. I want to move forward."

Casey pulled back to look her in the eyes. "Me too."

Amy shook her head. "I don't want you sleeping on the couch."

"You want me to go, now?" Confusion swept over Casey's face.

"No. New plan. I want you to come into the bedroom right now, and we'll figure out where to sleep later." Amy stood up, pulling Casey with her to the bedroom.

Once there, Amy saw the big, wide bed, and the enormity of where they were heading crashed in on her. She hadn't been with anyone in years. Darla had been the one to aggressively take the lead. Amy had always fallen into step with her.

Now, she wanted something different with Casey. But, was she ready for this?

"Are you sure about this new plan? Because we can go back to the old one." Casey must have seen the panic she was trying so hard to hide. Amy grabbed Casey before she could psyche herself out.

"Yes. Move forward, lady," she said, and pulled her onto the bed. Casey laughed, a throaty, musical laugh which chased most of Amy's misgivings away.

They sat for a moment just looking at each other. She had only known Casey for weeks, and yet Amy felt as if she had waited a lifetime for this moment. Casey must've felt it too, since she slowly lowered her lips to Amy's. Her kiss was soft and velvety. It rocked Amy's world.

Casey pushed her down and lay across her. Casey's tight breasts and long lean muscles pressed against her, soft here, hard there, and oh, so sexy everywhere.

Amy tingled all over. And then she decided to let go and let passion guide her.

"New plan," she said.

Casey's eyes widened as Amy rolled her over onto her back and straddled her.

Amy wanted control, to steer her own course. She tugged at the first button on Casey's shirt.

Casey moaned as her fingers slid from button to button. And then there was only Casey's warm skin and her perfect breasts. Her nipples were already erect and waiting.

Amy brushed her fingers lightly over their tips, and Casey arched in pleasure. She gently squeezed and tugged until Casey's breath was labored and she moaned softly. Amy moved from one firm peak to the other, teasing with her lips and tongue.

"No fair. I get to play too," Casey said.

Smiling, Amy sat up and pulled her own shirt over her head.

"God, you're so sexy," Casey said, tugging her bra aside and taking a nipple in her mouth. She teased her with her tongue and teeth.

It took them only a minute to shrug out of the rest of their clothes and lie naked side by side. Amy traced a finger down the curve of Casey's tanned hip. She held her breath as she touched her. Her fingertips explored Casey's taut belly and the softness of her inner thigh, and then, as they drifted closer to her center, she hesitated, unsure of herself. It had been a long time since she had been with a lover.

"Please," Casey begged, reaching to guide Amy's fingers toward her need.

Amy felt the heat, felt the dampness before she touched her there. To know Casey wanted her was all the encouragement she needed. She slid her fingers into her.

Casey moaned; her whole body went still, waiting.

Amy pushed again, past the soft folds, and found her swollen and ready. Her thumb glided over her clitoris, fluttering against it, sending a spasm of pleasure through Casey, driving her hips into a primordial rhythm.

At first, Amy moved with slow sensual strokes, building in tempo as she felt Casey's body tense around her fingers.

Casey pulled her into a deep kiss. She pushed her tongue impatiently inside Amy's mouth, and her growing urgency flowed in with it.

Amy pushed deeper as Casey rolled her hips against her, and they moved in unison as Casey's pleasure grew.

Casey dropped her head back and cried out over and over as Amy thrust deeper into her and the waves of Casey's orgasm rolled over both of them. Casey reached for Amy's hand, stilling it, pressing it to her, as they rode out the last few ripples of her pleasure.

She dropped back onto the bed. "Wow," she gasped. "If that's what moving slow is like, let's disengage the brake permanently."

Amy chuckled. "I think we already have. I know I have."

Casey's eyes sparkled. "Shall we try out that theory?" She pulled her into another kiss. Casey's passion and desire still steered the embrace, but there was something else simmering underneath that Amy couldn't quite place at first. Casey pulled back to look at her. Tenderness shone in her eyes, and Amy felt her heart melt. There had never been tenderness before.

And then the rest of her melted as Casey rained soft kisses down her neck, stopping at her breasts to nibble and suck. She swirled her tongue around her erect nipples. The kisses moving downwards, across her stomach and lower still. Amy shivered in anticipation as Casey's breath blew across her sex.

Casey drew in her scent before dipping her head down to her curls. She licked and nibbled. Just when Amy didn't think she could take the teasing anymore, Casey slowly slid her tongue into her. Pounding sensations, both physical and emotional, coursed through her. "Oh. Yes," she cried.

Casey's mouth was honey as she eagerly explored. She worked her way into places that Amy didn't even know existed and when she rolled her tongue over Amy's clitoris, a spasm of pure pleasure jolted through her. Casey dropped lower, plunging her tongue into Amy with swift, hard strokes. Amy groaned. Nothing had prepared her for how good this felt.

She clenched the sheets in her hands as Casey drove hard inside her. Casey added her thumb to the play and rolled it over her clit. A roar began in Amy's head as a whoosh of pleasure raced through her body. Her orgasm came hard and fast, exploding through her body. Casey took her clitoris into her mouth and sucked gently as the last sparks of orgasm faded.

Amy opened her eyes to see Casey looking at her with eyes brimming over with tenderness and care.

"No brakes," Amy said, breathlessly. "No brakes is good."

Casey laughed, and slid up the bed and into Amy's arms.

CHAPTER 10

AMY DIDN'T REMEMBER FALLING ASLEEP, but when she opened her eyes to the early morning, bright sun streamed through the window. Casey had flung a leg over her in the night, almost as if staking claim. Amy snuggled back into her, warm and happy. She closed her eyes again, hoping to fall back asleep, but the memory of Casey's lovemaking still tingled across her body, and suddenly, she was wide awake.

Idly playing her fingers along Casey's knee, she traced the angry scar, no longer red and new, but still jagged to the touch. Her hand moved slowly up Casey's thigh to the round softness of her behind. She rolled over to face Casey, who was still asleep. Amy's hips felt stiff, but the pain was a welcome reminder of the pleasure they had shared and of this wonderful change in their relationship. And as an athlete Amy knew the surefire solution to muscle fatigue was another workout.

Amy kissed Casey's collar bone. Lingering traces of citrus rose from her skin, but mostly it was all her. Amy found the scent intoxicating.

Her nipples brushed against Casey's soft skin, and desire flamed in her again. She began to nuzzle Casey's ear when a strange beeping broke her concentration.

"Don't stop." Casey pressed her sleepy body against Amy's.

"Shit." Amy sprang from the bed. "It's your phone."

Casey sat up. "Get it, quick. I left it on the coffee table."

Completely naked, Amy raced into the living room and lunged for the phone. Casey stretched out her hands for it, and Amy tossed it to her.

"Is it Rob?" she asked climbing back into bed. Casey swiped the phone and the screen leaped into life. Someone moved around in the downstairs den. At first Amy thought it was Tammy, but then Rob's bulky frame came into view.

"Holy shit," Casey said. "It's working."

"Oh my God, we've got him," Amy gasped.

Rob stood in the middle of the den, looking first one way, then the other, to make sure he was alone. Satisfied, he reached into the workout bag slung over his shoulder and pulled out the photograph he had stolen the day before. He carefully arranged it on the mantel as if it had always been there. With one last tap to the photograph frame, he hitched the bag up on his shoulder and headed in the direction of the gym.

"Hmm," Casey said thoughtfully, and pulled the sheet up so it covered her chest. "We got something at least."

"But what? What do we actually have?" Amy rummaged around in a chest of drawers for two clean T-shirts. She threw one to Casey who slid it over her body. The possibility of a morning dalliance had disappeared.

"I don't know. He's possibly stealing a photograph? Definitely messing with stuff that isn't his."

"That's not enough to go to Horowitz with. It's all circumstantial." Amy held up a pair of work-out shorts and when Casey nodded, she tossed them on the bed.

"I know. We got to find out if there's anything more."

"How?"

"For starters, we need to look in that bag."

"That didn't work out so well for either of us yesterday."

"I don't know." Casey, now fully dressed, gave Amy a long, hungry look. "From where I'm standing, I don't think it could've worked out any better."

Amy's face softened into a smile. "No morning after regrets?"

"None. You?"

"God, no." Amy didn't hesitate with her answer. She cocked her head. "Well, I do regret we can't jump back into bed and start all over."

Casey chuckled. "Me too. But we're moving forward, right? Now we need a plan B."

"Which is?"

"155...156...157..."

Rob grunted the numbers as he pounded out sit-ups. Amy stood in the doorway for a moment. His back was to her, his focus completely on the exercise, and his bag dropped carelessly on the ground. Amy could just take it and slide out of the gym, but she was part of a real team now. Better to stay with the plan.

She bounded up to him, timing it carefully so his back hit the ground when she loomed over him from out of nowhere and took control from the start. The thieving bastard didn't deserve any better.

"Hi! You're Rob, right?"

He flinched at her voice, "Yes."

"I'm Amy," she said, enjoying his response.

"I remember." His face fell and he sighed. "What can I do you for?"

"Well, you're a personal trainer and I like to swim. So I was wondering if you could come out to the pool and show me a few exercises I could do out there."

"I'm in the middle of a workout."

"Oh, it won't take long." She pouted a little for good measure. "Diego said you would love to.

I talked to him this morning. He says you would help me whenever I wanted."

"Diego said that?"

"Yep."

Rob grimaced and grabbed a white towel draped over a nearby machine and wiped his dripping forehead. "Fine. One really good exercise you can do in the water—"

"No. I was hoping we could go to the pool. To actually do the exercises."

"You're kidding?"

"No. I'm a doer. I learn by doing, not by listening. So it has to be out there." She gave her words the sing-song rhythm of one who is sure of herself.

"Whatever." He snapped his towel back onto the machine's handle.

Amy turned away with Rob following. Just as he seemed to be making a detour to his bag she slid her arm through his.

"This is going to be so much fun. You know, I want to get in really good shape for Diego." She dropped her voice to a whisper as she directed him out the door. "And our wedding night."

In the hallway, her shoulders dropped in relief. The rest was up to Casey. The heat had not yet become unbearable as she led Rob to the edge of the pool. She raised her face expectantly. "So the one really good exercise is..."

"Aren't you going to get in?" he asked. "I thought you were a doer."

She groaned silently as her own words came back to bite her. "Of course." She really had only one option if she wanted to give Casey as much time as possible. She turned to the pool and jumped in, fully clothed, feet first. "Okay, so the one good exercise is...?"

Rob stared at her incredulously. He looked so shocked she had to stifle the laugh that rose in her throat. She treaded the cool water, aware she looked absolutely ridiculous, and hoped Casey was having better luck rifling through his bag.

"The exercise?" she prompted.

"There's the Spiderman, where you climb the wall of the pool like Spiderman climbs up buildings. Stand at the edge, tread water with your hands and climb up the wall with your feet."

Amy, the doer, moved to the wall. "Oh, I like it. I can feel it in my core."

"And then there's one where you'll need a noodle." He kicked the bright purple cylindrical foam into the water. "Stand upright, press straight down on the noodle with both hands, and lean forward until you're on an even incline. That's it. Keep your head above water. Now stay that like that for two minutes."

Amy maintained the plank position and marveled that certified or not, Rob knew his stuff. The muscles of her stomach and back tightened and her sore hips loosened up. She fought the current of the water, as she actually tried to perfect the exercise.

Then, from the patio windows behind Rob's back she saw Casey slashing the side of her hand across her throat. Time to cut loose.

"Okay. That's great. Thank you." Amy released the noodle and it popped to the surface with a splash.

"You know two exercises aren't going to make Diego like you." Rob sneered down at her.

"Excuse me?" She flinched at the real venom in his voice.

"I know a couple more," Rob backtracked quickly.

"No. Two's good."

"Tell Diego I'll see him tomorrow." He disappeared inside without waiting for an answer.

Amy dog-paddled to the shallow end. Despite being able to run most people into the ground on the soccer field, she was not a good swimmer. She climbed out, water streaming off her clothes.

Casey slunk into the patio from the side gate. "He's gone?"

Amy nodded.

"What the hell?" Casey asked, laughing while Amy stood dripping all over the patio.

"I lied to get him out here, and then I had to jump in the pool to prove myself." Amy looked down at water running off her shorts and T-shirt and started laughing, too. "What'd you find in there?"

"Nothing," Casey said. "Nothing but sweaty, gross clothes, and towels that smelled like they've never been washed."

"Great. So I did all this for dirty laundry." She squeezed out her top. Water streamed to the flagstones.

"I don't know. I'd say turnabout is fair play. I can see why you pushed me in that first day..." Casey's gaze slowly roamed her body and goosebumps rose up on Amy's skin. "I finally get to see you dripping wet."

"I don't know. I was pretty wet last night." Amy blushed at her boldness but met Casey's look head on.

Desire smoldered between them, and suddenly, Amy didn't care about her wet clothes, or Rob's weirdness and his photoshopping.

Casey took a step toward her and then stiffened as her gaze drifted over Amy's shoulder.

"Hi, Diego," she called softly.

Amy spun around to see Diego, larger than life, striding out onto the patio. "Oh, great! You're here, Casey. You obviously got my text," he said.

Casey nodded, hiding her surprise.

Amy plastered a fake smile on her face. "You're back early. We didn't expect you 'til later." She cringed. Her first sentence and already a mistake. She should have said "I," not "we."

This was going to be too easy to screw up. Or maybe she wanted a way out? She pushed the thought out of her head as soon as it entered. Not possible.

"I flew back ahead of the team. I have great news!" Diego beamed and took her in his arms. He instantly recoiled. "You're all wet. What happened?"

"I... I..." For the life of her she couldn't think of a lie.

"I dared her to jump in with her clothes on." Casey saved her. Now she was treading the path of lies. "We were just goofing about."

"Okay. Glad to see you're having fun," Diego said dismissively. "Where's Tammy? I want to tell all three of you together."

"Let's go find her." Casey turned Diego back to the house and gave him a gentle push forward. Behind his back, she caught Amy's eye and mouthed, "You okay?"

Amy nodded, but she wasn't sure. Diego's unexpected arrival had given her the jitters. Whatever the news was, she could roll with it. But she wasn't ready to give up her precious, truthful moments with Casey for the lies of her public life.

Casey touched her shoulder in a quick caress and they followed Diego indoors.

Tammy came rushing out of her apartment into the kitchen with an apology already flowing from her lips.

"You're home. I'm so sorry. If I knew you'd be home early, I would've been ready. Give me a second." She cast Casey a withering look. "No one told me."

She flew into action, pulling the carrot cake from the pantry and making cups of coffee all at once. Amy stood under the air conditioning in her damp clothes, wondering if she could catch pneumonia in the middle of a heatwave. She should go up and change, but she was on the job now.

Casey sat down at the table and crossed her arms defensively across her chest.

Diego, oblivious to the women in his life and the way they felt about him and each other, stood easily at the kitchen island, beaming from ear to ear, chatting about the game and his goal.

Amy caught Casey's eyes once, and she dropped her head as Diego prattled on. Finally, they sat around the table with coffee and cake before them.

Diego reached out and cupped Amy's hand for show. "I'm bursting. I can't wait to tell you all."

They stared expectantly at him.

"I got the call," he said, his voice thick with emotion. "The national team. They want me at the training camp next week."

"Oh, Diego! That's amazing." Tammy jumped up and rushed to enfold him in a bear hug.

Casey was next in line with a kiss on the check and a simple, but warm, "That's truly wonderful."

Amy stood back from the rest watching until Diego circled her with his arms and dropped his head in for the kiss. Amy stiffened. It was only acting on both their parts. But now as his lips met hers she couldn't help but feel as if she were cheating on Casey in some bizarre way.

"Oh my God. You're really wet," Diego said as he released her.

"You should go change," Casey said, so sharply that everyone turned to look at her. "I mean she's dripping all over the floor."

"Sorry, Tammy. I just wanted to hear Diego's news." Amy apologized.

"No worries." Tammy said with uncharacteristic charity.

"Go change. I want to drive over to my mother's to tell the family the news. I already told her, but I made her swear that I could tell everyone else. Will you come with me?"

"Of course."

With a happy nod, Diego, her boss, released her from the kitchen. It took everything that Amy had, not to look at Casey on her way out, especially when she heard Diego issue all sorts of intricate instructions to her for a busy working day.

Isabella opened the door with a wide grin that mirrored her son's. She immediately took him into her arms with an excited squeak. "Gracias a dios, hijo mío! Te lo merecías."

"Don't jinx it, Mama. I haven't made the team yet." Diego laughed happily, but his tone suggested that in his mind he was already wearing the red, white, and blue of the national uniform.

"Come in. Everyone's here." Isabella stood back for them to enter. She cupped Amy's cheek as they crossed paths. "His good luck charm."

Nausea whirled in her stomach, but she managed a wan smile. This was so much different from the first time she had come here. Then she had been pretending to be someone that she wasn't; now she was pretending to be someone she didn't want to be. She wasn't entirely sure what the difference was, but clearly it involved a stomach that did flip-flops.

Luckily, the attention wasn't on her, and she managed to stay in the background, even sidling up to where Abuelita sat on her throne in the living room. The language barrier would ensure that she could disappear into her own thoughts, which were whirling around herself and Casey and their predicament. Who knew when or if they would have any alone time together to discuss how to manage the unmanageable.

When everyone raised a glass to Diego's success, Abuelita's bony hand reached for hers. She squeezed it lovingly. Amy fought back tears. She was the woman who had survived her parents' death without crying even once, and now this simple touch from an old lady was almost enough to send her over the edge? What the hell was going on here?

Abuelita squeezed her hand again when she noticed Amy's eyes filling up. "Qué lindo que sientes tanta emoción por eí."

Amy didn't understand a word of what she said, but got the tone immediately. Abuelita's approval came with another rush of nausea.

The afternoon couldn't end too soon for Amy, but Diego's family, who grabbed any excuse to come together, celebrated long into the afternoon. She allowed herself to look at her phone only twice. No texts from Casey. When the summer light started to fade in the backyard, Isabella asked, "What does everyone want on their pizza?"

Amy bit her lip rather than respond. There was no way she could choke down a slice with her stomach still rolling.

"We can't stay, Mama. We have that thing, right, Amy?"

Amy blanked. What thing did they have?

Isabella noted Amy's expression. "Don't make her lie, cariño. See how uncomfortable she is telling fibs for you? If you both want to be alone to celebrate, just tell us. We can take it."

"No it's not that, although it does sound tempting." Diego rushed the last part out almost too quickly. "Isn't your friend playing at the Roadhouse? Is that tonight? Did I get it wrong?"

"Simon? He is playing, I forgot all about that! We need to go. I mean I'd like to go, if you still want to." It was the last place she wanted to go, but she had the tickets in her wallet and it would get her out of this frying pan.

"You kids have fun tonight." Isabella directed them to the door. "Oh, Amy, are we still on for tomorrow? At your house?"

That's right. She wanted to come over to set the date for the wedding. "Of course, Isabella." Another thing to get out of.

In the car, Amy expertly stuffed her hair back down her blouse while Diego chattered on about his future. As she half-listened, she twisted the engagement ring she had put back on earlier. The big, fake diamond glittered in the street lamps that were just starting to flicker on. It felt heavy on her finger.

Diego shifted in his seat. "You know, maybe Casey can come out and join us. I need to go over that paperwork I asked her to get, and tomorrow I have a session with Rob and then practice with the Atoms. That wouldn't be too weird, would it? They've got tables there right?"

He wasn't really asking her, but Amy's heart soared anyway when she gave her answer. "A little weird, maybe, but you need to use your time wisely now."

"Yeah. We'll just have to make sure that whoever Paul sends out to take those Facebook pictures gets the fun part of the evening not the work part."

"We can totally make that happen." She would see Casey tonight after all. She stopped fidgeting with her ring.

The Roadhouse was right off the freeway just outside of the Los Angeles county line. It looked like nothing special from the outside: a big wooden warehouse with a dilapidated sign built into the roof and a huge, free parking lot. Amy wouldn't have given the place a second look if Simon hadn't talked about it non-stop from almost the moment she'd met him.

"You're either going up or coming down if you play at the Roadhouse," Simon had said at least a million times. The intimate club was known for booking the next great band before they hit the big time, and Simon had spent most of his few free nights there studying the acts. A gig here was his dream come true, and Knight had delivered on it. Simon must be over the moon. Maybe they could push the restart button on their friendship tonight? She'd love for that to happen. She was missing him too much.

"Who are you guys?" The middle-aged rocker at the front door gave Amy an appreciative look as he took the two VIP tickets from Diego's outstretched hand.

"He's the VIP," Amy said.

"Really? Who are you, dude?"

"Diego Torres."

"Who?"

"The pro soccer player?" Amy jumped in. The last thing she needed was a moody Diego.

"Cool, you know Pele?" The man's voice sounded like he had smoked way too many cigarettes.

"No. I've never met him."

"Oh." His gaze returned to Amy and lingered on her body.

"Where are we sitting?" Impatience crept into Diego's voice.

"Over here, dude." The man lead them through the standing crowd to a roped off section with tables and chairs. Their table was only a few feet from the stage.

"Here you go Mr...VIP."

"Look, we're going to need another ticket." Diego handed over a wad of cash. "Could you leave it at the door for a Casey Palmer."

"Um." Amy looked around the club. "Can we have that table over there?" She pointed to the one other empty table in the back of the VIP section. It was up by the bar. She wasn't sure of how Simon would feel about her coming here at all. And here she was, right in his face. She would hate to put him off his game on his big night. Besides, she was pretty fragile herself and hiding by the bar didn't sound half bad, especially if Diego wanted to sneak in some paperwork.

"That one's a restricted view. This is the one that's reserved for you. It's our best table." The man's face crinkled with confusion.

"Then we'll take it." Diego sat down as if he owned the place. "Two Perriers please. I'm in training," he added as if the man needed an explanation.

Amy sighed and joined him, twisting her ring as she sat down. The lights dimmed.

"Ladies and gentlemen, the Roadhouse is proud to present Plastic Zippers!"

Simon and his bandmates rushed onto the stage. Amy was close enough to see the excitement blazing from his eyes. He lifted up his guitar, stared into the audience and struck his first cord to wild applause.

Amy had heard Simon play countless times, but never with such energy or passion. Talk about moving forward. He'd found what he loved to do in life, and the crowd was eating up every note he played. At the end of the first song, they cheered loud and hard.

"Thank you! Thank you. Believe me, we're so, so happy to be here." Simon's English accent rang out over the sound system. The crowd applauded. He seemed to grow at least two inches on the stage as he surveyed the crowd with a smile a mile wide. Then his gaze hit Amy sitting directly below him. His smile vanished.

Amy met his stare and shrugged in a "how could I not come" way. His answer was loud and clear. Simon looked away as if he hadn't seen her at all.

The opening riff for the next song rang out, and Amy's heart dropped. This day was turning into a disaster.

"Maybe we should go." She turned to Diego, shouting to make herself heard over the music. She tugged at her blouse. The heat of all these people crowded together was becoming overwhelming.

"Why? Your friend's pretty good. And there should be a photographer here somewhere." Diego yelled back at her and slung his arm around the back of her chair. He took Amy's hand and dropped it on his thigh. His muscles were hard and strong and so very different from the sleekness of Casey's. She was like a panther to his bull. "Besides, we need to wait for Casey," he added.

Amy flinched in her seat, her nails almost digging into Diego's leg. Diego's mentioning Casey the exact moment she was thinking about her drove her deeper into her funk.

"I think I'm going to need a real drink," she said, looking around for a waiter.

The Roadhouse special, a frozen mojito, went down far too easily. Amy hadn't had anything to eat all day, and when the rum and lime hit her stomach, she sat back a little easier and let Simon's music roll over her. Booze. No wonder they called it liquid courage.

Amy spotted Knight's photographer before she'd taken her first picture. She might as well have had *I'm a plant* tattooed onto her forehead. She swung toward them with a cell phone sporting a fancy clip-on lens bigger than the phone itself. Amy smiled lovingly at Diego and dropped her head to his shoulder. Above them, on stage Simon spun on into a dance move that placed him close to their table. He took in their lovers' embrace with a face sour with resentment. And then Casey came through the door.

The club was crowded with standing room only outside of the fancy VIP seating area. But somehow Amy knew the moment Casey appeared. She felt her presence as a prickling sensation on the back of her neck, as if all her senses were on fire. When she looked up Casey was striding purposefully toward them.

Amy clamped her hands to her chair to prevent herself from leaping up and running into her arms. Simon, the heat of the club, the fake relationship with Diego, and now Casey, it was all too much for her little mojito'd brain to take. Way too much.

As soon as she saw Amy, Casey tilted her head in both warning and concern. When she arrived at the table, she thrust a plain white folder at Diego.

"Hi!" Diego shouted as he took the folder. "Thanks for coming up."

Casey stood lamely at Diego's side and looked across to Amy.

"Sorry, I don't think he could wait," Amy said. "He's really excited."

"Who could when their dream's within reach?"

"Down in front," someone yelled.

Oblivious, Diego rifled through his paperwork. "Is that all the national team and FIFA want?"

"Yeah. You need to sign here. And here." Casey pointed to two lines on two different pieces of paper, and when Diego patted all his pockets in vain, she produced a pen as well.

Above them, Simon registered disbelief as the loud conversation continued right in front of the stage. He glared at Amy and moved away to the other side of the platform.

Amy slid farther down in her seat. How much worse was this going to get?

"Is that it?" Diego asked, folding up the papers and stuffing them back into the folder.

"Paul just needs to send over your birth certificate to prove you're a US citizen. I don't have it. But yeah. That's it."

"Okay. I'm sorry you had to drive all this way."

Casey nodded but didn't move.

Diego looked unsure for a moment. "Do you want to join us?" he eventually asked.

"Yeah, thanks," she answered as she'd planned on staying anyway. Casey grabbed the only open chair and squeezed in between Diego and Amy.

Diego and Amy both had to scoot over as she wedged herself in. Casey's leg slid against Amy's as she sat down. The pressure was comforting, even though Amy wanted so much more. If she could just stay like this and let Simon get through his song list without any more disturbances, the night could still be salvaged.

The Plastic Zippers ran through their set. The crowd clapped and hooted louder with every song until Simon struck the last chord with a flourish. "Thank you very much," he told the crowd. "You've made our gig something special. I'll never forget tonight at the Roadhouse."

Amy willed him to look at her, but he jumped off the stage and walked right past her into the crowd that surged to meet him. He was soon surrounded by people slapping him on the back and shouting compliments.

"What's going on?" Diego asked, snatching up the folder that held his dreams as people pushed past their table.

"That's the gimmick here," Amy said. "The bands always hang out with their fans afterwards. The new bands cultivate a following, the fans can talk to their heroes, and the bar sells more drinks."

"Did you want to go say hello? Because I should get home. I start early in the gym tomorrow."

"Oh my God! Are you Diego Torres?" Knight's plant jumped to their side, playing the part of a thrilled soccer fan. She had ditched the lens and now held the bare cell phone out with a hand shaking, pretending excitement. Everyone close by turned to look at Diego, and some people drifted over.

"Who is he?" someone asked.

"He plays for the Atoms." Someone else had actually recognized Diego.

"I think he just got called up for the national team," the hired fan girl said conspiratorially to the couple next to her, who immediately passed it on.

"The national team!"

"Oh my God. He's so cute."

"Hey, can I have your autograph?"

"Excuse me." Knight's undercover girl literally pushed Casey out of the picture as she continued to snap candid shots of Amy and Diego surrounded by a growing group of fans.

Amy wanted to throw up when she saw the people around Simon ditch him as they raced to join the real celebrity sighting. Cell phones flashed as everyone jostled to grab a selfie with Diego.

"Knight must be having a wet dream wherever he is," Amy said out loud to no one in particular.

And then Simon was at her side. He stood there for a second silently watching Diego and his fans. He felt so comfortable and familiar that Amy turned around to tell him how much she had missed him.

The words where forming on her lips when Simon hissed, "You couldn't let me have this one night, could you? You know I've been working for this gig for years. And when it finally comes around, you have to show up with him?"

"Si, I...I need to tell you—"

"Forget it, Amy. We're done." He twisted away. She grabbed for him, but he shook her off. "Just fuck off."

Amy felt as if she had been slapped. He was absolutely right, though. As far as it looked to him, she had shown up on his big night, rubbed her happy relationship in his face, and then her boyfriend had stolen all his thunder. It was the last straw.

The dam that had been holding back her emotions cracked. Tears welled up in her eyes, and she fought hard to hold them back. Diego still posed for pictures, lost in his fans and his fame. She took a deep breath and searched for inner fortitude. Then her gaze lit on Casey. She stood so still in a room full of movement, her eyes dark with pain and concern. The dam broke and Amy raced outside into the summer night.

Blindly, she stumbled to the back of the building and wept by the trash bins, away from the people in the parking lot. She leaned her head against the stucco, the knobby texture pricking at the skin of her forehead, and cried for the first time since her parents had died. Tears slid down her face as she sobbed quietly against the wall.

Suddenly, arms wound around her pulling her into a loving embrace. The sweet scent of citrus enveloped her as she fell into Casey's arms.

Casey squeezed her tight, and Amy's sobs lessened. Finally cried out she rested her cheek against Casey's collar.

"You're all wet." Amy hiccuped, wiping her tears off the tanned skin she had been kissing only twenty-four hours before.

"Doesn't matter. Here." She was handed a tissue, and then another when one wasn't enough. "What happened in there?"

"I lost it. Simon told me to fuck off, and I just lost it." Amy wiped her eyes again and wondered how red and swollen they were. This was not the way she wanted Casey to see her on their second day together. Weak. Vulnerable. A mess. "Are you always so well prepared for damsels in distress?"

"Always." Casey tucked a strand of hair that had fallen over Amy's face behind her ear. "You want to tell me about Simon?" And when Amy winced, she added, "Or should we talk about it later?"

"What about Diego?"

"He left. Early day tomorrow. He asked me to apologize and take you home. Some boyfriend, huh?" When Amy didn't laugh, she tried again. "I get it. He's all wrapped up in the national team."

There was no bitterness in her voice, but Amy looked hard into her face to see what watching someone else achieve her dream was doing to her. And now, on top of her own hurt, she had to comfort a crying, insecure girl in a parking lot.

"I'm sorry for all this." Amy raised both palms in an apology.

"Oh, sweetheart." Casey cupped her cheek. "There's nowhere else I'd rather be."

Relief swept over Amy and her tears started again.

"Come on, let's get out of here. Let me take you home."

Amy followed Casey like a lost puppy. It wasn't until they rounded the corner into a group of people lighting up cigarettes that it occurred to her they probably shouldn't be walking so close together. She took a step away from Casey and scanned the parking lot to see if anyone was watching, like Knight's photographer or worse still, Simon. No one paid them any attention except for two middle-aged men who whistled and called for them to join them.

"In your dreams," Casey said lightly and continued walking to an old, tricked out jeep without sides or top. "Your carriage, my lady."

Amy looked around for the blue Camry. "Whose car is this?"

"My brother's. I didn't have a car, remember? I left it when I came over last night." She hopped in and threw a hand out in invitation to the passenger side. "It has the worst gas mileage ever, but it's fun on a warm night like tonight. Get in."

Amy did, fumbled for the seat belt, and held on to the handle on the glove compartment as Casey bounced down the canyon roads taking them back to Diego's house. She tucked her hair expertly down her blouse so it wouldn't blow around her face as the wind whipped around them. The warm wind fluttering around the windshield soothed her swollen face and eyes, or maybe it was Casey's hand on her thigh that soothed the rawness that enveloped her heart. She settled into the high backed seat and sighed deeply.

They drove in comfortable silence for a while until Amy began talking. The story about Simon tumbled out from the very beginning when Amy had met him online at a site for connecting roommates. Then on to working together at the Valley Arms, and finally the deal with Knight and Horowitz and his storming away from her at the club tonight. She told it clinically as if she were an unbiased witness to a crime rather than one of the chief participants.

"You need to tell him," Casey said when Amy had finished.

"Tell him what? That he didn't earn his own success? That I grabbed an easy way out of a dead-end life and pretended I was doing it for him? That no matter how easy the lies are, someone is always going to get hurt?" Amy dropped her head. "He doesn't want to hear any of that. And more, he doesn't deserve to hear any of that. It's easier, and better, for him if he just thinks he found success on his own and I'm just an asshole."

Casey pulled the jeep over onto the shoulder of the road under a big Californian oak. The moon streamed down through the branches and dappled soft light on to the hood of the car. She took both of Amy's hands in hers. "You are not an asshole."

Amy fought back a new round of tears. "I know. But I've been pretending in one way or another for so long, even way before Diego, and I don't know if I can do anything else."

There, she'd said it, and aloud, and not just in her own mind. She steeled herself for the response.

"Yeah, I know a lot about lying and pretending things are okay. It's not a good place to be." Casey squeezed her hands. "But you're not in that place anymore. What do you think yesterday was about?"

"Lust," Amy said simply.

"Yes." A sly smile creased Casey's lips. "And so much more. I don't know about you, but it felt really, really good to be active and involved in something other than my own problems for once. I felt like I was ahead of the game, not chasing after the ball."

"It did, didn't it?" Amy squeezed her hand back. Another thought rolled around in her mind, forcing its way out. "Casey, I think I'm

done with all this. All the pretending and lying."
She rushed on so Casey wouldn't think she was
talking about her. "I hope you're okay with it,
but I got to get out of this thing with Diego, and
Knight, and Horowitz, no matter what it costs."

"Okay with it? I'll help you do it. We're in this
together, right?"

They both leaned in for a kiss to seal the deal.

CHAPTER 11

"OF COURSE, YOU'LL GET MARRIED in our church, but the reception should be somewhere romantic. Full of fairy lights and flowers. Surely, you've been thinking about all this. Where do you see your reception?" Isabella asked Amy.

Amy swallowed hard. The early morning sun flooded in making the kitchen too bright for such an intense conversation. Amy and Isabella sat drinking coffee surrounded by a dozen wedding brochures that Isabella had dropped casually on the table when she had arrived. Now they lay like tiny land mines, ready to explode at the slightest touch.

"Um." Amy had no idea how to answer such a loaded question.

"This one's unbelievable." Isabella filled the silence by handing her a picture of a garden full roses and twinkling lights. "And it's right by the church, so it's really convenient. Usually you have to book a year in advance, but I know the director. So maybe we can get you and Diego in early. What do you think?"

I think I want to run screaming from the room. This was insane. Only last night she had told Casey she was getting out at any cost, and here she was, twelve hours later, discussing her wedding reception.

"I think Diego should be in on this conversation. I'll go get him." She jumped up before Isabella could stop her.

The steady clank of weights led her right to the gym. The door was wide open, and Diego sat on a bench with a free weight curled in his hand while Rob adjusted his elbow.

Amy hesitated, hovering in the doorway, uncertain what to do. The scene inside felt so intimate that it almost pushed her physically away. The men didn't even notice her.

But then a new emotion took hold of her. She wanted to rush in between them and rescue Diego. She didn't trust Rob one bit. But Rob made his move before she could make hers.

He dipped his head and kissed Diego full on the lips.

Diego dropped the weight with a thud and leapt away. "What the hell?" he yelled. "What are you doing?"

"Come on, Diego. You know you want it. I see the way you look at me."

"I do not." Real horror rose in Diego's voice.

"Who do you think you're kidding? We both know that you aren't into that skanky girlfriend." Rob moved toward him.

"Get the fuck away from me, man." Diego swatted Rob's hands as he reached out for him.

"We don't have to tell anyone."

"You'd better leave right now." Diego rose to his full height, anger and panic sparked off him.

"Seriously, man. This doesn't excite you?" Rob yanked a glossy photo out of his sports bag and thrust it at Diego. Amy couldn't see what exactly was on it, but from Diego's horrified expression, she knew it was one of the pornographic ones. He dropped it as if scalded.

"We could have so much fun, man." Rob's voice was full of yearning. He wasn't giving up. He wasn't even listening.

"Get the hell out of here and don't ever come back." Diego shoved him away. "You're fired."

"It's not going to be that easy. Since day one, your eyes have been glued to my ass."

Amy saw a hardness settle on Rob's face. A switch had flipped somewhere in his head. He grabbed Diego's crotch. "I can take all of you, if you let me."

Then Diego did something that Amy didn't know he had in him. He hauled off and slugged Rob smack in the face. It was like a scene from a movie. Rob fell to the ground and Diego stood over him, shaking with anger, eyeing him like the trash he was.

"Fine. I'll go." Diego strode to the door. He flinched when he saw Amy in the doorway, but he didn't stop and strode past her.

"Diego! Wait!" She attempted to grab his arm, but he shook her off and kept going.

"You'll be sorry!" Rob sounded almost as if he was crying.

Diego rounded the corner of the hallway into the kitchen. There he skidded to a sudden halt. Amy rushed in to find Isabella standing at the table.

"Diego? Was that you shouting? What on earth is going on?" She wore the expression that all mothers reserve for errant boys.

"Why are you here, Mama?" Diego could barely get the words out.

"The wedding, of course. Come join us. If you're done shouting, that is?" she said, lightly. Amy could see it was the last straw for him. Landmines had exploded under him all morning.

Diego's hands began to shake, and he clenched them into fists. "Not now, Mama. I—"

"Diego. Stop. You can't do this anymore." Amy heard herself say, much to her own surprise. The words just popped out.

He spun to her. "Amy..." His warning was soft, but very clear.

Amy's heart started pounding. If she went ahead, there was no coming back. But what had Casey said last night? "Get ahead of the game, not behind the ball."

"She's going to find out some way, Diego." Amy marveled at how confident she sounded. "The question is do you want her to find out from the tabloids or some internet scandal? Or from you?"

Diego said nothing. Panic rolled off him in waves. Amy had boxed him into a corner. Now he had two options, lie or come clean.

"Find out what?" Isabella asked quietly.

"Tell her. She's your mother."

There was a long moment where no one said anything, or even moved. Then Diego's whole body sagged, and Amy knew that she had finally reached him. His fists unclenched.

"I...I..." He raked a hand through his hair. He looked to Amy, who nodded her encouragement,

"This is as much for you as it is for your mother," Amy said.

"What is it, son?"

Diego sighed deeply and rushed his next words out. "Mama, I think I like men."

Isabella's eyes went wide, and she sank down into the chair reaching for the armrest to steady herself. So many emotions rushed across her face, Amy couldn't unscramble them all. Finally, she dropped her gaze to her hands. Diego waited with baited breath, and his nervousness reached across the kitchen to grab Amy. When Isabella finally looked up, a fierce determination had settled over her features. "I know."

Both Amy and Diego sighed almost in unison. Amy bit her lip to prevent a smile of triumph. She had called it. Isabella had known all along.

"But you two have an arrangement, right?" Isabella asked.

Now Amy started in surprise.

"An arrangement?" Diego echoed her thoughts.

"Sure. Where you go out and do...whatever you need to do, but you always come home to Amy in the end. You'll get married and there'll be grandchildren and family vacations and a life outside of that other...issue?"

Shit. Amy hadn't seen that coming. Isabella had known about Diego, but she thought that this thing with her was real too.

"No, Mama." Diego's voice was low and sad. "We're not going to get married."

"Why not?" Tears sprang to her eyes. "You're great together."

Diego pursed his lips and shook his head. "She's just a beard. I pay her to be my girlfriend. Amy's helping me out so I can keep my endorsements. This whole thing's a farce."

Another long silence. So long Amy wished she could turn back time so she and Diego could take it all back.

"Okay." Isabella rose, and started to gather up the brochures on the table. With something between a choke and a laugh, she let them drop back on the table. They scattered, the swish of paper deafening in the silence. As was the click of her heels as she moved to the door without a word. There, she paused for a moment and a sliver of hope ran through Amy. Would Isabella say something to salvage the situation, or at least give Diego some hope for the future? Surely she could step up and be the bigger person whatever she felt about Diego's sexuality?

Diego closed his eyes waiting for her next move. Finally, Isabella raised a hand to pat his shoulder but froze an inch away from touching him. She couldn't let it drop onto him. She turned and left without a word.

"That's it, then." Diego stiffened as the door shut.

"No, it's not." Amy moved toward him, until she saw the pain in his face and stopped short. "She'll come around." Her voice had lost the confidence from before.

"Maybe, but for now it has come between us." He rubbed his chin in despair.

"Diego, I am so sorry." And she was. It was ironic. She would have given anything to have had this conversation, no matter how heartbreaking, with her own mother. Diego would always have the honesty of this day to fall back on, whatever happened next.

"Fuck!" Clearly he wasn't there yet. "I was so stupid to think I could control all this. Or let Paul do it for me. First Rob, now my own mother. I am so totally screwed!" He stormed for the door. "I can kiss the national team goodbye if this gets out. This is all your fault!" A minute later, Amy heard the deep rumble of his car as it flew out of the driveway.

Amy felt a familiar churning in her stomach. This job was going to give her an ulcer. He was right on some level. Her advice had pushed him forward, maybe faster than he could cope with. Could she fix it? Yes, she thought she could, and she would start with Rob.

She rushed back to the gym, but it was empty. Rob was long gone. No evidence remained of the crazy drama that had unfolded a short time before. Except for a corner of a photo peeked out from under the leg press machine. It was the fake porn picture that had pushed Diego over the edge. Rob must have forgotten it in his rush to get out of there, or left behind it in some twisted attempt to get to Diego.

She flinched at the image. Diego and Rob were naked. Diego held out his erect penis as Rob went down on him. It was a horrible forgery. Their heads were obviously patched on to fake bodies, but still the overall impact was aggressive and sordid. Diego was right; Rob was crazy. Who knew what he might do next?

Her phone beeped. It was a text from Knight. *Rob's called a meeting. Can't get a hold of Diego. WTF is going on? GET IN HERE ASAP!*

A stab of pain shot through her stomach. Man, Rob was fast. What was he planning now?

Her fingers flew as she texted Casey. *Urgent. Meet me at Horowitz's now. Bring your phone.*

Jenna leapt up as soon Amy came through the doors.

"Ms. Kimball. Were we expecting you? Do you have an appointment?"

"An impromptu one. Upstairs." Amy marveled at the control in her voice.

"Ah...I'll just check on that." Jenna grabbed for the phone.

"Don't bother, Jenna," Paul Knight appeared behind Amy. "Amy has an appointment. I'll take her up."

Amy watched his eyes settle on Jenna's chest before he took Amy by the elbow and directed her to the elevator. Once inside she shook off his grasp.

"Do you want to tell me what this is all about?" Knight hissed at her. "Do you know why Rob called this meeting?"

"No. But this is what you get for meddling in someone else's life just so you can get a few bucks."

"What? Rob is coming over for reasons he won't disclose after you were investigating him. What did you do?"

"Me?" Amy's voice cracked. "You're pinning this all on me? After you told me to go after him? This is not my fault." It was then she knew with all certainly that come hell or high water she was getting out of this arrangement today. No matter what.

Horowitz's secretary, Rachel, greeted them as soon as they stepped off the elevator.

"Mr. Knight. Ms. Kimball. Good morning."

"Is he in?" Knight tilted his head back toward the corner office.

"Yes. But he's not happy about this sudden meeting."

"Neither am I." Knight threw a livid look at Amy. She bit her lip. The pressure was mounting. Casey had better get here soon.

"Can I get you a coffee or tea?" Rachel asked.

"Latte for me, Rachel." Knight headed for the glass door at the end of the corridor.

"And a latte for me, too. Thank you so much for making it." She met Rachel's gaze, and the older woman titled her head almost imperceptibly. "Actually could you bring me two? Someone else is joining us."

Horowitz was in a mood. His jacket hung over the back of his chair. Several crumpled balls of legal pad paper lay around the trash can.

"Did you find out what this is about, Paul?" Horowitz thundered as soon as they opened the door.

"No, Miss Smarty-Pants here hasn't said a word."

"I've solved the Photoshop mystery." She shrugged. Let them suck that up.

Horowitz stopped scribbling and gave Amy his full attention. "Well, young lady, who's behind it?"

Rachel arrived with their coffees.

Amy waited for her to leave.

"Are you actually going to tell us something?" Knight butted in before she could speak. "We're not here for the coffee. This isn't Starbucks, you know."

Amy's heart started thudding in her chest. Without Casey and her ammunition there was absolutely nowhere to go with this. She opened her mouth to stall when the office door whooshed behind her.

Rachel escorted Casey in. She looked crisp and businesslike in a soft, yellow blouse and gray slacks. She managed to look fresh and sharp, despite the hot day and the bad-tempered meeting.

"Finally. Let's get started. This better be good," Knight said.

Casey was shown to a chair, and Rachel departed.

Horowitz shrugged back into his jacket and made the meeting official.

"Casey, show them the video of Rob in the den," Amy said.

"Okay." Casey picked up her lead and ran with it. "You want good? This is the best."

Knight stood so close to Casey as the video played that eventually she rolled her eyes, gave him the phone, and moved over to Amy.

"I got you a coffee."

Casey took the cup Amy offered and fixed her with a look. "What's with the video?" she asked softly. "We don't have enough on Rob. I thought we agreed last night you were going to demand to get out of the contract."

"A lot has happened since then. I'll tell you later," Amy said. "You look great by the way." Having Casey by her side made her feel she could actually pull this off.

Knight slapped the phone against his palm when the screen went dead. "Okay. Who's going to tell me why we're watching Diego's trainer play with some shit on the mantel?"

"If you look closely, Paul," Amy said, "you'll see that he isn't playing with stuff on the mantel. He's putting back a framed photograph of me and Diego, and I bet an altered version of it has already arrived at this office." She looked at Horowitz.

He and Knight exchanged glances. Horowitz pushed a button on the phone. "Rachel, can you please bring in that envelope I sent down to... processing."

"That's what you call it?" Amy laughed.

Rachel appeared seconds later with a tan padded envelope addressed to Diego Torres by care of the law office. Horowitz slid the picture out and showed it to Amy. "You mean this one?"

The background was exactly the same, perfect snow-capped mountains, but in the foreground

Diego had his arm slung lovingly around a handsome man. Amy hated to admit it, but somehow he looked happier in this incarnation.

"Yes."

"Okay, so Rob's behind all this. But we need real evidence, because what I see here wouldn't stand up in court," Horowitz said calmly.

"I want out of my contract." Amy cut to the chase.

"What?" Knight said.

"Stop talking, Ms. Kimball." Horowitz inclined his head to Casey.

"Too late. She already knows."

"That's a major breach." Horowitz stared at her.

"Not if I deliver the evidence. The kind that stands up in court and stops Rob in his tracks. In return, you tear up my contract. Believe me, Diego will want it that way as well. I'm surprised he's not over here demanding it right now." She shrugged. "I'll give you two weeks' notice. Diego and I can break up any way you want—within reason, of course. I can be the bad guy, take the fall, and Diego can come out smelling like a rose. Maybe his popularity will spike?"

"No way. This isn't what we bought from you." Knight took a threatening step forward. Casey bristled, ready to defend Amy if needed.

Amy put a hand on her arm holding her back. "I'll keep everything I know a secret. Look, I just can't do it anymore."

"Why?" Knight asked. "Is this about money? Do you want more?"

Amy looked at Casey and tilted her head in an unspoken question. Casey nodded.

"No, it's about her." She slid her hand down until their fingers intertwined. Chances for happiness didn't come around all that often. "I want her."

"And she's already got me. So you better say yes, because you have no leverage," Casey added, squeezing Amy's hand tight.

Knight plopped down on a chair, completely deflated, his anger rushed out of him. "For Christ's sake. You have got to be kidding me."

"Well, if I am, your joke is my reality. Do we have a deal? The contract in exchange for stopping Rob in his tracks? I can stop the blackmail or whatever he's up to."

"We could always do our own investigation, Ms. Kimball." Horowitz's tone wasn't dismissive, though. He looked at Amy with real respect.

"You could. And probably do it better than I can. But can you do it in five minutes? Rob's on his way, and I have direct evidence." The phrase jumped easily to her lips; the one pre-law class in college wasn't a total waste after all.

"She's got us by the short hairs," Knight said sorrowfully to Horowitz.

"Yes. She always was a little too smart for this game, and we need to put those pictures to bed more than we need to put Diego in bed with her," Horowitz said.

"Agreed. But I don't like her running the show." They talked over the heads of Amy and Casey as if they weren't there.

"Let's see what she's got," Horowitz disagreed. "But we're not going to tear up the contract until we have a full confession." Horowitz expression turned steely as he pinned his gaze on Casey. "There's my leverage, young lady."

"Okay. That's fine," Amy said, hoping that she sounded surer than she felt. The rest of the plan was decidedly less solid than what had just transpired.

As they waited for Rob to arrive, Rachel fetched the contract in question which Horowitz ceremoniously placed in the center of his blotter. He then picked up the phone and spoke in quiet tones to someone giving explicit and lengthy directions. Knight sat sulking on his cell phone, leaving Amy and Casey to their own devices. They drifted over to the huge glass window that overlooked the entire Valley.

"Can you really stop the blackmail?" Casey leaned in close. "Did you get something else?"

"No, I lied, and I'm going to have to keep on lying if this is going to work." Their heads touched like a couple of schoolgirls whispering during a class lecture.

"Isn't that exactly what we're trying to get out of doing?"

"I know. You're right. But at this moment a lie to be able to live the truth seems like a fair trade," Amy said, though her thoughts rolled the opposite direction. She knew that lies had a way of exploding right in the liar's face.

"Does it?" Casey asked. "Are you sure that's a trade you want to make?"

"I don't know. But this whole thing has always been so messed up. And now Diego's MIA. That's why we have to get out. Can you think of a better way?"

Casey shook her head in reply.

The door flew open.

"I'm suing Diego Torres for assault!" Rob's entrance was aggressive. He banged the glass door so violently it jammed open. The unflappable Rachel trailed after him.

"Mr. O'Brien," she announced as if Rob had just entered a ballroom, "and Mr. Wallace."

A greasy, little man trailed after Rob. He wore a cheap polyester suit and a bad comb-over.

Rob pointed to a purple bruise that was just starting to form around his eye. "Look what he did to me. You think he's going to be able to ignore me now?"

"Please join us, Mr. O'Brien. And Mr. Wallace, you are?" Horowitz came out in front of the desk offering Wallace his hand.

"I'm representing my cousin. I mean Mr. O'Brien. I'm his attorney." They shook, and Wallace puffed out his chest. "I'm afraid we have a very sticky situation on our hands." He was getting off playing with the big boys.

"And it's about to get even stickier." Horowitz leaned against the desk, giving Amy the floor. "Your show, Ms. Kimball."

"Hello, Rob." Amy began haltingly. The antagonism on Rob's face threw her.

"Why are you here?" he snapped. "Haven't you done enough damage?"

Oh, we're just getting started. She slid the doctored picture of Diego out of the envelope and held it up. It shook in her hand. Rob was going to have to take them the last few yards himself.

"I've never seen that picture before in my life." He crossed his arms.

Amy let out a breath she didn't even know she was holding. Rob had shown all his cards with his choice of words. He had exposed his jugular, and now she had to go for it.

"I think you have. I think you stole the original, created this, and then sent it to these gentlemen here."

"Where's your proof?" He was belligerent, unware of the trap closing in around him

"Casey?" Casey had the video clip set up and cued. She played it for Rob and Wallace. Amy didn't watch the screen like everyone else. Her gaze was riveted to Rob's face. She observed him flinch, and when he saw himself pull the framed photograph out of his bag, he paled. When the video clip ended Amy let the reality of the situation settle on him for a moment.

"You're lying when you say you haven't seen that photograph before."

"I haven't seen that photograph before." He persisted in digging himself in further by pointing to the picture in her hand. "All you got is that I look at Diego's stuff and sometimes carry it around with me in my bag when I'm at his house. You can't prove I take anything off the premises." He shrugged. "Okay, so it's weird. Last time I checked, being weird wasn't illegal." He glanced over at his cousin who had the audacity to wink back.

Amy dropped the photograph back onto Horowitz's desk. The moment was here. All she had to do now was tell one simple lie to trap Rob. The problem was that regardless of whether it worked or not, just by telling it, she joined the ranks of Knight and Horowitz. Liars by trade and choice. Her lie was for a good cause, but the second she said it out loud she'd be no better than they were.

The real truth, which had been circling around her for weeks, landed hard in her thoughts. There was no easy way out for any of them. Parents died, knees tore apart, the men you loved didn't love you back. Casey was right: everyone had a hard luck story. She needed to grow up and realize that as difficult as the next couple of minutes would be for her and Rob, this was the only way out. For all of them.

Amy looked over at Horowitz, who watched her with real encouragement. She threw a quick glance at Casey who nodded back. Finally, she turned to Rob who was shaking his head back and forth, firm in his denial.

"You don't have anything on me. And, frankly, Diego's the one in the hot seat and he's going to pay." He touched the bruise on his face.

"Come on, get over yourself, Rob. You know I saw you both in the gym today."

Fear flooded his eyes.

"Yeah, and guess what?" Amy pushed on before she could back out. "We had a camera down there as well. So if anyone's going to sue anyone, it's Diego, suing you for sexual assault!"

Rob recoiled as if he'd been punched in the face for the second time that day.

"Is this true, Rob?" Wallace shrank about an inch as his chest caved in. "You didn't tell me any of this. What'd you do?"

"He kissed him. And grabbed at him in places that no man should ever grab another man. We have the video."

"Yeah, so what! I didn't do anything that he didn't want!" The muscles in his legs tensed.

"Shut up. Don't say another word." Wallace issued the command.

Amy pulled out the other glossy photo, the one she'd found in the gym. "And we have this. You showed him this to freak him out. You wanted to blackmail him, Rob, didn't you? It sure looks like it."

"No! It wasn't like that at all." Rob went beet red and started shouting. "It's all your fault!" He rushed at Amy with both fists raised. Amy shrank back, her heart pounding.

"Stop!" Wallace cried.

Horowitz leapt to defend her, but Casey got there first. She simply stuck out her foot and Rob sprawled to the ground face-first.

"You okay?" Casey asked her.

"Yeah." She looked down at Rob on the floor.

The anger that had come on so quick had left him. He sat up, more than a little shaken. "All I wanted was Diego." His voice was broken.

"You never even had a chance, Rob," Amy said. He was all sorts of crazy, and Amy almost felt sorry for him. She was about to get her happy ever after; he wasn't.

"We'll drop the assault case," Wallace weighed in quickly. "But I assume that you want to make another kind of deal about the pictures?"

"Play your cards right and work with Mr. Horowitz. He'll make you a decent deal, Rob. That's what they do here," Amy said.

"We'll get to that. Believe me, it will be worth your while to cooperate. But first tell us the whole story." Horowitz's voice was gentle. The man had some guile.

Rob said nothing.

Wallace pulled him off the ground and back into a chair. "Don't ruin this, man. You still owe me for that thing with your mother."

"Fine." Rob cupped a palm over his other eye. He was going to have matching shiners. "At first, I doctored the pictures only for myself. It was fun. Sort of fantasy stuff. No one was ever going to get hurt. But the longer it went on, the more obvious it became that Diego was in denial, and that got me mad." He looked up, anxiety filled his face. "Not mad enough to harm him. I'd never do that," he said. "I thought if I sent the pictures here, it might force him to accept who he really is. He's not for you, Mizz. Thing," he spat the words out with real venom. "No matter what he tells you at night up in your little room. He likes men. I know we would've been happy together, but I never got the chance." He looked over at the photo lying on the desk. "All I wanted was to make him look at himself. Really look. I was never going to do anything else with the pictures."

"We can make sure of that." Horowitz pushed the speaker on his phone. "Rachel, could you take Mr. Wallace and Mr. O'Brien to the conference room while we draw up the paperwork?"

Rachel ushered them out, and suddenly it was over.

Then why am I still shaking? Casey was by her side in a heartbeat. "Get the contract," she said.

"My turn," Amy said, pointing at her own folder sitting out on the desk.

"Yes. It is." Horowitz grabbed the contract from the folder.

"Wait! You sure we can't convince you to stay on?" Knight asked. "The money is very easy here."

"No. I'm good."

Horowitz tore the contract into two pieces with a theatrical flourish and fed it to his industrial paper shredder. Knight groaned as each piece of the contract was eaten up.

"I'm impressed how easy that was, Ms. Kimball. If you ever think about going to law school, drop by afterwards." Horowitz said.

"Are you kidding? In two weeks, I am done with this world forever."

She headed for the door without waiting for Rachel to escort them out.

"You did great!" Casey said as they waited by the elevator. Her breathing had returned to normal.

"You had to rescue me again," she said. "First the pool, then the concert, and now Rob."

"We make a good team. We each play to our strengths."

"I look forward to exploring that more now that I am free." The doors opened to their new future together. "But first I have to find Diego. Make sure he's okay."

In the end, it was Diego who found her.

Amy and Casey went back to his hacienda but the house was empty, so Amy texted him; Casey texted him. Even Tammy texted him. But no one received a reply.

Casey returned to her office to get some work done. Amy went upstairs with Dulce at her heels as usual. By late afternoon, a soft knock came to her door. Amy opened it, expecting Casey, but a sheepish Diego stood on her doorstep. He put both hands over his heart, looking contrite.

"Look, I'm so sorry about earlier," Diego said. "I was upset, for so many reasons, and I took it all out on you."

"No. I get it. The whole thing was intense. Did Paul tell you? It's over for real now. There is no more Rob."

"He did. And he also said that I have you to thank for that."

"Well, it was the least I could do. Do you want to come in?"

He nodded, reached down to pick up Dulce, and rubbed his face in her fur. "Hey, pup."

"Where were you?" she asked when they were settled on the couch with two beers. Diego was breaking a lot of rules today.

"The track. At UCLA. It's where I always go when I am upset. I ran for hours. Trying to work all of this out. But I guess you were already doing that for me." He reached over and took her hand. "I know this day would have ended up much worse if it weren't for you."

"You talk to your mom?" Her hand felt odd in his.

"No. It's too fresh. We both need to get over our disappointment about this morning."

"It's a start, Diego, like little baby steps. But don't leave it too long."

He squeezed her hand and dropped it. "It doesn't matter as long as I got you by my side. I'll go off to training camp and give the national team my absolute best shot."

"Paul didn't tell you?"

"Tell me what?"

It dawned on Amy that Knight had left her to tell Diego that #Amiego only had two weeks to go. She broke it to him gently.

"I thought you liked it here." He looked genuinely confused and hurt when she was done.

"I do," she said.

"And I thought you liked me." He acted as if they were really breaking up.

"You're a great guy, Diego, and this is probably the best job I will ever have. But that's the problem. I don't want this kind of job. In the beginning, I thought it was all about the money and the fun of brushing up against the MLS and you. But you see, I'm not getting anything real out of it. I know that this is working for you, it's just not working for me."

"So what would be real for you?" He set his beer down and gave her his full attention.

"You're not going to believe this. And I'm in no way making fun of you. So I'm going to pull the band aid off fast. I'm gay, too. Casey and I are together, and I don't want the fake you and me to get in the way of something real with her."

"Casey? My Casey?" His eyes went wide with surprise.

"Yes. She's my Casey now. But I'll share her with you on work days."

"Wow." He raked his hand through his hair and stared at her. "That's a lot to take in. You two are serious?"

"I think so. I hope so." A tinge of panic rose. They hadn't had time to talk about what they both wanted. Everything had happened so quickly. She thought she knew Casey's feelings. The joke would be on her if she had made all these changes for Casey, only for her to tell her that what they had together was a fling.

But even if she and Casey didn't work out, she suddenly realized that by sitting here telling the truth, she was way ahead of the game. Her panic evaporated as quickly as it had come. Whatever happened now, whether she was with Casey or not, she was definitely moving forward.

Silence hung between them. Diego rubbed his chin. And then he threw back his head and laughed. A great big hearty laugh full of happiness.

Amy flinched. She wasn't sure of this new development. She had expected annoyance, anger, maybe even a little regret, but not a belly laugh.

"Diego, are you okay?"

"Okay? This is perfect." He grabbed both her hands this time and shook them with delight. "This is why you should stay."

"Sorry?" Confusion played over her face.

"You know, I thought maybe...Boy, do I feel stupid now, but I thought that you were developing feelings for me."

Amy shook her head. "No."

"See? That's great." Diego's voice was full of relief. "And now that I don't have to worry about that or taking advantage of you. This totally puts us on an even footing. Plus, you're with someone I trust completely. We should totally keep all this going. It's been really good for my image." Diego was actually getting excited about the idea.

"Diego I—"

"—and, frankly, my game is fantastic now. Being a couple has really taken a weight off my shoulders. I haven't played this well in a long, long time."

"Okay, but you see—"

"Amy, I'm not ready to give you up, and I'm going to fight for you."

Amy almost toppled over. Again, the last thing she had expected Diego to say. They almost sounded like a real couple.

"Diego, I'm flattered, I think. But—"

"It comes down to this. I need you. How about I get Knight to double your salary?"

"It's not about the money anymore."

"That's even better. Then do it for me. A good deed. Give your and Casey's relationship a little positive karma?" He looked at her with puppy dog eyes. "Please?"

"I don't know." The resolve with which she started the conversation seemed to evaporate. It suddenly seemed awfully selfish to leave Diego in the lurch like this. "I'll talk about it with Casey. I'll get back to you after practice tomorrow, okay?"

It wasn't until she was walking across the flagstones to Casey's office that she realized two things. First, it had been a very long time since there had been anybody in her life to run things by. And second, cool air swirled around her as she moved.

The heatwave had broken.

CHAPTER 12

CASEY DROVE AMY TO A park at the edge of the Valley. It was nothing special, but it was the one place where she said she felt the most comfortable. A basketball court stood at one end with a covered toddler playground at the other. In between was a large grass area where kids of all ages scooted around with soccer balls at their feet. Every square inch of turf was marked out into practice grids. Amy and Casey sat and watched the activity.

"This is where my first team practiced. We met here twice a week when I was growing up." Casey pointed to a spot not far from them where a female coach encouraged her girls into a three-man weave. "There were days I spent more time here than at home or even at school."

"You miss it?"

"I do. Every day. But my turn's over, whether I want it to be or not."

A girl, around Mia's age, finished the weave with a blistering shot into the pop-up goal.

"Wow," Casey said. "Look at that shot. That girl's got a foot on her. It'll be her turn next.

And then someone else's after her. The game's in good hands." She snuggled into Amy. "And, besides, there are lots of ways to move forward."

"What are we going to do about Diego?" Amy raked her teeth over her bottom lip. "I should just tell him two weeks, and that's it. Right?"

"I don't know. He'll be right in the middle of camp then," Casey said.

"That's what he said. And I get it, this isn't all about us. So I wait until after camp, until the decisions come down? What if he doesn't make it? Or worse, what if he does? He and I stay together until after the World Cup?"

"I don't know. That does seem a little extreme."

"And what happens to us in all that time?" Amy asked.

Casey shifted on the bench so she could look into Amy's eyes. "Who knows?"

Amy's heart clenched.

Casey touched her arm reassuringly. "That's not what I meant," she said. "What I meant is it's impossible to have this kind of conversation two days into a relationship. Who knows where we'll be in two years or even two months. But we're putting it all out on the table here? Yes?"

Amy nodded, unable to speak, her throat suddenly dry.

"Okay." Casey took a deep breath. "This situation is so crazy, but you know, life is like that. We'll figure it out, and I'm pretty sure we'll make it work. And if it doesn't, we'll turn it into a situation that does work for us. We're both athletes. We know how to see a play before it develops, right?" Amy nodded, unsure of where this was going. "The bottom line is that whether you're Diego's fiancée or not," Casey looked straight at her, "I'm all in."

Amy squeezed her eyes shut; the relief hit her hard.

"I'm all in, too." As soon as she said it, Amy realized that this was her new truth and all the rest with Diego and Knight and Simon, none of it mattered as long as she had Casey.

"So if we're good with each other, where's the harm in helping Diego?" Casey asked.

"I worked way too hard to get out of that situation to walk right back into it." Already all the pretense and lies were starting to weigh on her shoulders. "I know it doesn't look like it from the outside, what with all the parties and the promos and the VIP boxes at games. But it's getting really hard to hold it all together."

"Who says you'll walk right back into it? I say you go in with guns blazing completely on your own terms."

"Which are?"

"That's for you to decide."

Amy settled back on the bench. It felt good, for once to be in the driver's seat.

Knight almost leapt through the phone when she texted him. *Can we meet?*

He responded, *I'll meet you anywhere you want.*

They ended up in the bowling alley coffee house and hammered out a new deal with no contract and no penalties. This one was very much in Amy's favor. She got everything she wanted. She would have reduced appearances with Diego, the wedding date would go into a permanent hiatus, and both she and Casey would get an all-expense paid trip to the World Cup, if that panned out for Diego. Top of the list, however, the homework–soccer club would progress from a study to a reality at top speed. They hemmed and hawed only over one point.

"Take it or leave it," Amy said. "It's non-negotiable. I'm done lying and so is Casey."

"It opens us up to a lot more liability. I don't like it."

"Yeah, I know. But you're going to have to trust me. And if you don't trust me, you're going to have to trust Casey. She really loves Diego, you know, and will make sure that nothing comes back to bite him. She's the one you should have gone to in the first place, anyway."

Knight slumped back in his seat. "Everyone hates a Monday morning quarterback, you know."

Amy tried not to smirk. Instead she wrapped her hands around her coffee. "Well, you in or not?"

"I had a call from Nike today...and Diego wants this. It all depends on how far he is willing to go," Knight said.

"And if he agrees?"

"Then I'm in. But I have to tell you I don't feel good about it."

The smirk she had been holding back burst out. "Welcome to my world."

Amy and Casey walked up the wooded streets of the Hidden Hills complex. Diego, along with Dulce, had joined them. Wide dirt paths opened up before them in the moonlight, weaving like ribbons around the huge mansions on the hillside. Dulce ran along beside them, her backside wagging in ecstasy as she followed one scent after another into the surrounding wild chaparral.

Casey and Amy had met Diego as soon as he arrived home from practice, and then under the thin pretense of all of them taking Dulce for a walk, they quickly left the house. Amy saw a curtain flutter in the kitchen window as Tammy watched them head up the driveway.

"So?" Diego said, as they turned the corner onto the hiking path by the house. "Are we breaking up or getting back together?" He didn't smile at his own joke. Amy could see the tension in his face.

"The answer's up to you," Amy said. "Casey and I want to be together. But we don't like leaving you high and dry, especially if you think having a fake fiancée is helping your game."

"It is," Diego said, cautiously, a little hope appearing in his eyes.

"Okay, so what we would like to propose is that Casey and I come out to the people that matter around us, and you and I still present ourselves to the public as a couple."

"As my fiancée?" The hopeful look grew stronger.

"As your fiancée, but with no set date for the wedding. The Atoms' season will be over soon, and hopefully you'll be away with the national team. So it won't be as intense as it is now."

"So where's the catch? That sounds great."

"Here's the catch. You're not going to like it, but hear us out." Amy looked to Casey, who gave her an encouraging nod. "Casey will tell her family about us. Tammy will have to know, since Casey will be around a lot more."

"Okay."

"But for all of us to really be happy, you have to make it right with your mother."

"No." Diego spoke so sharply that Dulce whimpered. "I've thought about this almost non-stop since it happened. She knew, and yet she never said anything to make it easier for me."

"Maybe she didn't know how to. It's not an easy subject to broach." Amy thought of her own unresolved past.

Diego said nothing, but his legs churned a little faster up the hill that they were climbing.

"Diego, wait," Casey said, grabbing his arm to pull him back. "Take it from me. You can't go off to training camp carrying any demons with you. Believe me, I know. Everyone thinks that I played in that scrimmage because I was loyal to UCLA, but the truth is I was scared. I was terrified I wasn't good enough, and I went balls out in that game to prove something to myself, something that frankly, I didn't need to prove. Their goalie took me out, that's a fact. But the real truth is that I took myself out way before I even walked out on that field."

Amy caressed her shoulder. The tense muscles softened under her touch, but Casey's gaze bore into Diego. He was not going to escape.

"I'm really sorry that it didn't work out for you, Casey. So very sorry. But we're not the same, you and I." Diego shook his head and turned to go back up the hill. Casey detained him again.

"Our demons are different, for sure. But you're fooling yourself if you think you don't have any, and they aren't affecting your game. Just look at these last few months."

He shook off her arm, but didn't move away. "I know," he said softly, "that's why I want Amy to stay."

"But this conversation is about more than Amy. In the end this is about you and how you play the game. And I'm not just talking about soccer."

Amy stepped up. "Remember what you told me that first night together out on the patio? How nice it was for you to have someone around that you didn't have to pretend with? Imagine if that wasn't a paid position. Imagine if that person really, really loved you as a mother loves a son."

"I don't think I can. It's just too hard to face that disappointment again. I mean, if there was someone, I might think about it. But there isn't. All I want right now is a ball at my feet and a red, white, and blue jersey on my back."

"This might help you get there," Casey said.

"This feels a lot like an ultimatum," Diego said.

"That's what it may feel like, but really it's a chance to grab a little bit of peace. The weight will be off your shoulders, and you can suit up for the national team feeling free and clear. Chase away those demons."

"Lies can eat people alive," Amy told him. "Trust me on that. But it's still your choice."

"You're not firing me, are you?"

"Tammy, I have to..." Diego began. The seriousness of the coming conversation crept into his voice

"Oh my God, you are firing me!" Tammy jumped up and pointed a finger at Amy. "It's because of her, isn't it?"

Casey burst into laughter. "In a way. But it's not what you think."

Tammy's face turned bright red. "I knew it. The second she walked in this door, I knew something was up. You wanted to replace me from the beginning. Didn't you?"

"No, that's not it at all," Amy said, and threw a look at Casey that told her to behave.

"I'm sorry." Casey choked down her laughter.

They all looked to Diego, who screwed his mouth up to speak, but could get no further. The last time he came out, it had been a disaster. Amy knew for so many reasons he needed a success story and hoped Tammy would be it. She nodded her encouragement to him.

"Tammy, I need to tell you..." he faltered. Tammy sat in the exact same seat as his mother had. The coincidence of that was not lost on Amy.

"He wants to tell you that you're his only girl." She finished the statement for him.

Tammy's eyes narrowed in suspicion, and then popped wide in delight. "She's leaving?" She looked directly at Amy. Her excitement gave her voice a lilt that almost made it attractive.

"No." Diego tried again. "What we mean is I don't like Amy in the way you think."

"I don't understand." Tammy looked back and forth between them; obviously thinking she was being played.

"Let me try to explain." His words came in fits and starts as he launched into the explanation of the true nature of Amy's and Casey's new relationship, and the way he personally fit into it.

"They like each other and I...I...like men," he said wrapping up the long, rambling speech. It took Tammy only a moment to comprehend his full meaning.

"Hah!" Tammy flew to Diego's side pulling him into a hug and kissing his cheek repeatedly. "So I am your only girl."

"Yes, yes." Diego laughed, full of relief. He gently prised Tammy off him, patting her on the shoulder. Tammy's eyes changed from rounded amazement to her usual adoring gaze, and Amy could see Diego was more confident in himself after the reception he'd received.

"So what can I do to help?" Tammy asked. It seemed Team Diego had one more player.

Two days later, Diego stood in front of his mother's house, anxiously wiping his hands on his pants leg. Nervousness played over his face as he went to ring the doorbell. His finger hovered over the button.

"You're sure about this?" he asked one more time.

Casey and Amy stood on either side of him. "It went well with Tammy," Casey said.

"Yes, but Tammy's not my mother." Diego's anxiety pulsed out of him.

"No. But when your mother accepts you for who you are, it will feel even better." Saying it out loud made Amy believe it a little more, but they all knew they were taking a big chance here.

"Okay. Here goes nothing." Diego hit the button with his usual take-no-prisoners attitude. Isabella opened the door. Her eyes were guarded, but she stepped aside to let them enter.

"Come into the kitchen, Mama." Diego led the way, as Casey and Amy disappeared out into the backyard as agreed. The air out back was cool enough to be comfortable, and they took seats under the shaded patio. Amy crossed her fingers on her left hand, as she had every time she had taken a corner kick in her college career. She knew from experience that set pieces only went well when everyone did as they should. Isabella was like a temperamental forward. Would she step up when asked?

Casey reached over and took her hand, and Amy shivered at the touch. They had spent several nights together in her bedroom, and their game had only become better and better, the more they practiced.

"If this goes badly, I'm not sure Diego will recover," Amy said.

"I know. But we have to let it play out."

"How'd your parents take it?" Amy asked.

"Well, I told them I liked girls when I was ten, so they had a long time to digest it before I started dating. They're fine with it now. Actually, I think they're more worried about my financial future and what I do for a living, than who I date." Casey squeezed her hand. "I haven't told them yet, but I'm sort of thinking of med school. It feels like it's finally time to face my future. What do you think?"

"I think it's great. Will I have to call you Dr. Palmer?"

"Only in bed."

Amy stifled a giggle. It seemed rude to sit outside laughing while Diego was inside having the hardest conversation of his life. Instead, she focused on Casey's hand resting in hers, wondering at how it had almost become an extension of herself. A moment of silence hung between them.

"You don't think we forced him into this, do you?" Amy suddenly asked.

"You would think so the way he's been whining about it. But you've seen him play; he's a force of nature. He wouldn't be in there unless he wanted to. He just needed a push."

"I hope so."

"Of course you do. You love Diego," Casey said.

"Wow. I guess I do."

Casey pulled Amy's hand into her lap. There was something very easy and casual about the movement, almost without thought, but it spoke volumes. Diego wasn't the only one she loved, but it was too soon to say it. Maybe even too soon to feel it, but she was moving that way for sure.

"You know who's going to be super excited about us getting together—besides me, of course? Mia." Casey answered her own question. "Let's tell her next."

"I thought she wanted you to be with Diego."

"Diego? Oh my God, no. She thought we were together. That's what made her so upset at the golf course. I think she may be following in my footsteps in a lot of ways, if you get my meaning."

"Really?"

"Yep. So are you ready to take on the job of role model as well?"

"Um..."

"You said you wanted to work with kids."

"Yeah, but as in teaching literature or helping them with homework, not guiding them through a lifestyle I know so little about myself."

"I think you're doing pretty well," Casey said.

"That's because we're doing pretty well."

Just then Amy heard the patio door slide open. She went from comfortable and loved to flat out guilty in a heartbeat. She untangled herself from Casey and stood up to face whatever had happened inside. Casey jumped up with her, presenting a united front.

Diego stepped outside, his face stoic, but he looked as if he might have been crying at one point.

"How did it go?" Amy asked.

"She went to her room. She said she couldn't come outside."

"But how'd the talk go?" Amy pressed him.

He shook his head. "Good, I guess. I don't know. We talked more about how hurt we both were. That I didn't trust her enough to tell her in the first place and that she didn't help me through something so difficult when she knew all along. Come to think of it, we didn't really talk about wanting to be with men at all."

"That's a great sign," Casey said.

"You think?"

"Yes. You'll get through the hurt, for sure," Casey said.

"I hope so. She actually kissed my cheek before she left."

"See, that's the best sign yet."

"Although there's that whole Catholic thing she needs to get around, and the fact that there will never be a church wedding. And I need to know that she really has my back, no matter what comes next. Like a boyfriend, someday. I hope." Diego nodded slightly. "That's a real possibility thanks to you two, but first there's a lot to deal with for both of us."

"The first step is always the hardest," Amy said.

Diego rolled his eyes slightly. If he were on the verge of being able to joke about all this, Casey was right, they hadn't forced him into anything.

"It's a cliché because it's true, you know," Amy said and looked straight at Casey.

"Well, there's nothing cliché about this truth," Casey said, "A man, his fiancée, and her girlfriend."

They all laughed, even Diego, who stood a little straighter as he did.

Casey had meant it as a joke, but it occurred to Amy that life in general was messy like this—lies and truth rolled up together so tightly that often it wasn't clear where one began and the other ended. Just like the three of them.

"Come on," Diego said, "There's this place down the street that serves stuffed poblano chilies to die for. Fresh shrimp, crab, and salmon, if we're lucky. My treat." He led the way with his long stride. Diego was never down and out for long.

Casey inclined her head after him. "You ready for hashtag Camiego?

"You bet. But at home, when we are alone, it's all about hashtag Casamy."

"Agreed." Casey leaned in for a quick kiss. Her eyes shone brightly; the chill was so long gone that Amy could hardly remember what it felt like.

"I'm going to enjoy creating that pretend Twitter account." Amy kissed her back.

Laughing, they followed Diego out, and into a future of their own making.

EPILOGUE

"I STAND IN FRONT OF you today proudly wearing our national team uniform, because a lot of people helped me along the way. But I am even prouder to pay it forward and to be a part of giving your children a safe and healthy place to come after school." Diego raised his arms to encompass the small crowd and the warehouse they all stood in. "But most of the credit goes to someone very special to me, without whose vision the Torres Academic Soccer Club would never have become a reality. Let's all give Amy Kimball a hand for keeping us on TASC!"

The crowd applauded and surged toward Diego as he jumped off the makeshift stage. Amy, standing at the back, gave Diego a big thumbs-up, and he blew her a kiss. She grabbed it out of the air like she always did, and marveled that somewhere along the way the action had become a natural and loving one between them.

Amy savored the moment as she took in the transformation of the warehouse. It had been a shell of a building when Knight had found it months ago. Now colorful USA Soccer and

Atoms' banners hung on the walls, and the radio blasted from huge speakers hung throughout the rafters. Parents grabbed applications at a corner table while their children ran screaming with laughter around the homework stations that Amy hoped, at some point, would support quiet study. Horowitz and Kane had donated several computers and printers, so there was actually a real chance the work would get done.

"Oh my God. You've got to try these. They're amazing." Casey delivered a plate of soft tacos into Amy's hand. "Where'd they come from?" She motioned to the husband and wife at the tacqueria cart outside on the small soccer field, who were assembling the tacos as fast as they could.

"Isabella found them somewhere."

"Of course." Casey nodded. "Oh my God, try the carnitas."

Amy looked for Isabella in the crowd. Full of smiles, she was helping the parents with the application forms. No one had been as gung-ho about TASC as Isabella. It was the vehicle that had brought her back into the center of Diego's life. They had slowly come together over the worthy cause, and had found they'd never left each other's hearts. Amy knew that this was a sign for all the good this place could do.

The first few chords of a very familiar song pounded through the warehouse radio. Amy's throat closed up. The music on the radio faded as the announcer cut in. "Get ready for the new release from the Plastic Zippers. Their latest, 'Unfriended,' is zipping up the charts."

"Did he ever respond to the invitation?" Casey asked quietly, so no one could overhear.

"No."

"I'm sorry."

"Me too." The day would have been one hundred percent perfect if Simon had been here too, but their wrecked friendship was the price of her lies. Simon was her payback, and it broke her heart to lose him like this. She gave Casey a loving look, thankful that they, at least, had made it to the other side intact.

"Muchas gracias, mija." A soft voice whispered into her ear. Amy turned to find Isabella beside her. "This is a wonderful thing for the community and for him...for us. Thank you for taking down the wall between us. I never knew it was there until you came along." Her gaze shifted to her son, who was in the middle of an adoring throng.

"You're welcome. I'm glad it worked out."

"Worked out? That's an understatement. Did he tell you he's the starting forward in next week's qualifier?"

"Only about a million times." Casey laughed. "He's playing great."

"Well, I hope that he's thanking you for that, too. He couldn't have managed without you. Both of you. Now we need to work on getting him a...a boy..." Isabella wasn't quite ready to finish the phrase out loud, but Amy was pleased at how hard she was trying.

"Someone special." Casey rescued her. "And that will take time."

Amy threw her a grateful look. Casey jumped to everyone's defense. That was just her way.

Diego slipped out of the group and moved toward them. "What do you all look so serious about? This is a celebration."

"Nothing," Amy said. "We're just happy."

"Mama?"

"Nothing. We were just chatting, cariño. But now that you're here, I think that when you do settle down with...someone special—"

"Mama, I'm all about the soccer right now." Diego blushed. He was struggling with this new version of himself as much as his mother was.

"I know. But when you do, I hope he shares a lot of the same qualities with this one." She wrapped an arm around Amy. "Or this one." She wrapped the other arm through Casey's. "You're lucky to have friends like this in your life."

Diego smiled. "I know. I could do a lot worse."

"What I'm saying here is that you couldn't do much better." Isabella was becoming flustered but determined to speak her mind. "So when you're ready to think about children, think about having them with these two."

"Mama!"

"What! It's not unusual for a woman of my age to have thoughts about grandchildren."

"Slow down there, Isabella." Casey laughed.

Amy said nothing. The idea was too soon, for sure, but this unlikely group, as messy and strange as it was, was her family now. Having children and bringing even more love into this family at some point didn't sound half bad.

She met Casey's gaze and mouthed the words she had been wanting to say for so long, "I love you."

"I love you too," the answer came back, equally silently.

Moving forward. Sometimes it took you places you didn't even know you wanted to go.

###

ABOUT CATHERINE LANE

Catherine Lane started to write fiction on a dare from her wife. She's thrilled to be a published author, even though she had to admit her wife was right. They live happily in Southern California with their son and a very mischievous pound puppy.

Catherine spends most of her time these days working, mothering, or writing. But when she finds herself at loose ends, she enjoys experimenting with recipes in the kitchen, paddling on long stretches of flat water, and browsing the stacks at libraries and bookstores. Oh, and trying unsuccessfully to outwit her dog.

She has published several short stories and is currently working on a second novel.

CONNECT WITH CATHERINE:
Website:
catherinelanefiction.wordpress.com/
Facebook:
www.facebook.com/profile.
php?id=100004577749399
E-mail:
claneauthor01@gmail.com

OTHER BOOKS FROM YLVA PUBLISHING

www.ylva-publishing.com

BITTER FRUIT
Lois Cloarec Hart

ISBN: 978-3-95533-216-7
Length: 244 pages

Jac accepts an unusual wager from her best friend. Jac has one month to seduce a young woman she's never met. Though Lauren is straight and engaged, Jac begins her campaign confident that she'll win the bet. But Jac's forgotten that if you sow an onion seed, you won't harvest a peach. When her plan goes awry, will she reap the bitter fruit of her deception? Or will Lauren turn the tables on her?

BARRING COMPLICATIONS
Blythe Rippon

ISBN: 978-3-95533-191-7
Length: 374 pages

When a gay marriage case arrives at the US Supreme Court, two women find themselves at the center of the fight for marriage equality. Closeted Justice Victoria Willoughby must sway a conservative colleague and attorney Genevieve Fornier must craft compelling arguments to win five votes. Complicating matters, despite their shared history, the law forbids the two from talking to each other.

HEART'S SURRENDER
Emma Weimann

ISBN: 978-3-95533-183-2
Length: 305 pages

Neither Samantha Freedman nor Gillian Jennings are looking for a relationship when they begin a no-strings-attached affair. But soon simple attraction turns into something more.

What happens when the worlds of a handy-woman and a pampered housewife collide? Can nights of hot, erotic fun lead to love, or will these two very different women go their separate ways?

DAMAGE CONTROL
Jae

ISBN: 978-3-95533-372-0
Length: 347 pages

When actress Grace Durand is photographed in a compromising situation with a woman, she fears for her career.

She hires PR agent Lauren Pearce to do damage control, not knowing that she's a lesbian.

As they run the gauntlet of the paparazzi together, Lauren realizes how different Grace is from her TV persona.

Getting involved would ruin their careers, but the attraction between them is growing.

COMING FROM YLVA PUBLISHING IN 2015

www.ylva-publishing.com

ALL THE LITTLE MOMENTS

G Benson

A successful anaesthetist, Anna is focused on herself, her career, and her girlfriend. Everything changes abruptly when her brother's and sister-in-law's deaths devastate her and her family. Left responsible for her young niece and nephew, Anna finds herself dumped and alone in Melbourne, a city she doesn't even like. She tries to navigate the shock of looking after two children battling with their grief while managing her own.

Filled with self-doubt, Anna feels as if she's making a mess of the entire thing, especially when she collides with a long-legged stranger. Anna barely has time to brush her teeth in the morning, let alone to date a woman—least of all one who has no idea about the two kids under her care.

Just when Anna finally starts to feel as if she's getting some control of the situation, the biggest fight begins and Anna really has to step up once and for all.

DELIBERATE HARM

J.R. Wolfe

US soldiers Portia Marks and Imma Thoms found love during the second Iraq War, after Imma, a combat surgeon, saved Portia's life from a roadside bomb. Immediately inseparable, the two of them returned to civilian life engaged and followed Portia's postwar dreams to Zimbabwe, where they brought humanitarian aid to the struggling nation. But when Imma is arrested on false charges and executed for trying to escape prison, Portia returns home to Chicago bereft, numbing her grief by day with work and by night with alcohol.

Until one night, Portia is stopped by a stranger in the street who tells her that Imma actually escaped death and has been on the run ever since. But before Portia can find out anything else, the man is killed before her eyes.

Unable to dismiss the chance that Imma may be alive, Portia turns to two old friends from her Army days, now in the CIA, to help her find out the truth. Her search leads her to Zimbabwe, then to South Africa, and finally to London. Along the way, she stumbles upon plots within plots involving not only the People's Revolution—a radical terrorist organization—but also the CIA and a mysterious Russian crime syndicate.

When Portia discovers that the People's Revolution has a dirty bomb that they plan to set off at a highly public event somewhere in London, her search for her fiancée becomes a race against time.

The Set Piece
© by Catherine Lane

ISBN 978-3-95533-376-8

Also available as e-book.

Published by Ylva Publishing, legal entity of Ylva Verlag, e.Kfr.

Ylva Verlag, e.Kfr.
Owner: Astrid Ohletz
Am Kirschgarten 2
65830 Kriftel
Germany

www.ylva-publishing.com

First Edition: June 2015

Credits
Edited by Gill McKnight & Anna Genoese
Cover Design by Streetlight Graphics